THE CASE OF THE
APPRENTICE
IN THE
WINDY CITY

Michael W. Drwiega

The Case of the Apprentice in the Windy City

Michael W. Drwiega

Copyright © 2024 by Michael W. Drwiega

Published by 1st World Publishing
P.O. Box 2211, Fairfield, Iowa 52556
tel: 641-209-5000 • fax: 866-440-5234
web: www.1stworldpublishing.com

First Edition
ISBN Softcover: 978-1-4218-3556-3
LCCN: Library of Congress Cataloging-in-Publication Data

CONTENTS

The night Professor LaCroix went missing, she agreed to rejoin her friend Marla Davis within two hours of their departure from the Gold Room. This among other facts Detective Poblano determined with admirable dispatch. What troubled Robert was his mentor's rush to suspect Sánchez as lying behind LaCroix's disappearance. The textbooks warned against first impressions that could bias or retard an investigation. When he gently mentioned this, however, the veteran sleuth only scoffed, noting that one needed more than "classroom" logic to make it as a private investigator. Success required the right intuition, a feel for how the world worked, and sound judgment grounded in experience—the kind of hard, practical, sometimes gruesome experience Joseph Poblano had racked up plumbing Chicago's most dangerous neighborhoods. Feeling rebuffed, young Robert curbed further comments, yet doubts would haunt him till the very end.

SATURDAY MORNING:
A CASE
MORE CURIOUS
THAN IT SEEMED

"I was still in bed when she called," Poblano said. "It took a shake from Gloria to convince me I wasn't still asleep having a bad dream."

The call to Poblano had indeed come early, around half past five that morning. Robert checked his phone: It was now 9:24. Summoned to work unexpectedly, the young man had rushed to his mentor's downtown office, catching a train at the Bryn Mawr stop. He'd had no time to appreciate the sun rising over Lake Michigan on that first Saturday in May. He'd had no time to think of the sunshine warming the beaches along the lakefront or glinting off the tops of the cars rolling in both directions on DuSable Lake Shore Drive.

"She sounded frantic," Poblano went on. "You know how women can get." Occasionally gesticulating, the detective stepped one way then the other behind his desk, seldom glancing at Robert, speaking as if he were talking to himself.

His desk had a computer on one side and a photo of his wife Gloria and their five children on the other, the children aged 9 to 20. A three-and-a-half-foot by four-foot poster photo hung on the wall behind the desk depicting the Magnificent Mile at night. In the photo, the skyscrapers with all their windows lit looked like gigantic fluorescing honeycombs towering above Michigan Avenue.

"Marla Davis found me online about a year and a half

ago," Poblano was pacing behind the desk, talking to himself. "She wanted me to investigate a suspected theft on campus, keeping the matter confidential unless the culprit could be positively identified. She had no hard evidence. As it turned out, I never did find a thief. In the end, I doubted that a theft had even occurred."

Robert's ears perked up. In an armchair facing the desk, he'd been avidly jotting notes down on a clipboard in his lap, terrified of missing anything that might prove to be significant. "You couldn't determine if a theft had even occurred?"

"That's right," Poblano stopped pacing and stared at him.

The seasoned investigator had a spooky Italian look, Robert thought. *Like some of those Mafia characters on television.* Appearing as sharp as any corporate lawyer in a suit and tie, his thinning hair slicked back along the temples, he had a nose somewhat large albeit not bulbous and lips seemingly habituated to curling into smirks. Of average height and no obvious athletic prowess, he nevertheless possessed a brawny build that would have made him a bull in a street fight. His most striking feature, though, was his eyes. Dark. Potentially expressive. Unnervingly penetrating when he wanted them to be.

"That's *right*," he repeated, fixing his eyes on Robert, causing the young man's heart to thump. "Davis claimed that some of her papers had been stolen—something having to do with a grant proposal. I thought she was overreacting. I thought I might have been hired by a paranoiac. But you know something?" His eyes grew large. "She proved to be right. At least to an extent.

"Months after I dropped the case, campus security found the 'lost papers.' They were in the possession of an elderly professor, a George Hamilton, I believe. The old guy had taken them by mistake, mixed them in with some of his own papers, and forgotten about them."

Robert smiled. *The absent-minded prof!*

"As a result of that experience, I wouldn't say now that Davis is making a mountain out of nothing. There might be a mole hill in there somewhere. Nonetheless…"

Robert looked up from the clipboard. Poblano was rubbing his chin. Whether he was admiring the job he'd done that morning, getting in a good shave despite hurrying to get to work, or simply mulling something over, the young man couldn't tell. "I suggested that LaCroix might simply have changed her mind. About going out to eat, I mean.

"There were a group of them. Six or eight academics. They were all going to meet at the Berghoff after the conference. If LaCroix changed her mind, maybe she thought it unnecessary to inform anyone as, in such a large group, she would probably not be missed. But Davis insisted something was wrong."

"Maybe she knows something," Robert timidly suggested, "something she's not telling."

Poblano went on talking to himself, following his own line of thought. "She knows LaCroix. They're friends. She can tell when something's wrong, she said. But still…" he turned to Robert, knitting his brows to show how flummoxed he felt. "I can't afford to go running after everyone who drops out of touch for a few hours."

The young man nodded. Poblano, facedown, began pacing again behind his desk like a distracted fighter measuring the dimensions of the boxing ring in which he was expected to perform. "They attended a professional conference at a hotel.

In the Gold Room. I've seen that place. A nice place. Seats a few hundred people."

Robert had never seen the Gold Room but he had no trouble picturing it: a palatial convention room, the kind they have at posh hotels like the Hilton or the Hyatt. He pictured the place packed with professors and graduate students; men in suits and ties; women in business skirts and high heels; all seated on fold-up chairs in rows from front to back, attentively listening—or pretending to listen—to a panel of scholars behind a table on a dais.

"After the conference, Davis, LaCroix and others agreed to meet at the Berghoff two hours later—enough time to change into more comfortable attire. Enough time also for LaCroix to take a taxi to her office at the university. She wanted to pick something up. A book or an article—Davis didn't know exactly.

"When she failed to show up at the restaurant, Davis tried to call her but got only voice mail. She left the restaurant early and went back to her condo. Couldn't sleep. Kept trying to call LaCroix. Then she remembered me."

"If she was that worried, why didn't she call 911?"

"I think even she knows the dispatcher would say she was overreacting."

"Why not the non-emergency number, then?"

Poblano stopped pacing and impaled Robert with another one of his hitman stares. "Have you ever had a girlfriend?"

Robert paled slightly, appalled at what anyone in his generation would have regarded as the impropriety of the question but also suddenly, uncomfortably aware of his slender, light-boned physique, and a sense of dread shuddered through him. *Did he strike Poblano as possibly...*

"Sure," he said. "Sure, I've had a girlfriend. Maybe not at the moment, but yeah, I've had one or two."

"Then you know that a woman in distress sometimes isn't thinking straight. Davis sounded hysterical. And I guess I would be, too, if I thought what she was thinking."

Robert waited for a follow-up and when none came, he asked, "What was she thinking?"

"That her friend's been kidnapped."

Kidnapped! The young man sat up a bit straighter, the skin tightening around his face. As a private investigator, he had expected to handle cases involving petit larceny, unpaid debts, cheating spouses, and background checks. *But kidnapping?*

"Wha... what do *you* think?"

"I think Marla's been watching too many soap operas."

The young man chuckled, masking the very real thrill that was rippling in the pit of his stomach.

"I tried to talk her out of it. Why would anyone kidnap a university professor? It's not like she was working on the Manhattan Project."

"What *was* she working on?"

Poblano shrugged. "Who knows? She's in the poly-sci department. Both she *and* Davis."

Robert recalled the reason LaCroix was returning to her office—to retrieve a book or an article. *Could that be a clue?* He tucked it away in memory as a question to be pursued later.

"Is she married?" he asked.

"You mean does she have a rich hubby? No. Nor does she have a rich father. Both her parents and all her siblings died in a car accident over twenty years ago."

Robert bowed his head. "Sorry to hear that."

"I am too. But let's not go off on ridiculous tangents. I doubt that kidnapping has anything to do with LaCroix's absence. I think Davis is on the hysterical side. But I'd also like to maintain good relations. Women talk, especially with each other, and my best advertising is word-of-mouth."

Poblano bent down to pick up his briefcase. "Gloria and I had planned to take Tommy and Sam to the Field Museum today. They wanted to see the big dinosaur."

"You mean Sue?" Robert referred to the over forty-foot-long *Tyrannosaurus rex* skeleton at the museum.

"Yeah," Poblano released a wistful sigh. "I really wanted to see the old girl today. With the boys. They'll be inconsolable."

Robert hurried his clipboard into his briefcase and stood up. "Where are we going?"

"To the university. For a little enlightenment."

* * *

Davis would have met them at Wilkinson Hall, but she needed to address an urgent family matter and, regretfully, had to cancel. Using the room number she provided, Poblano and Robert had no trouble finding LaCroix's office at the north end of the third floor. It was what they discovered *at* the office that threw them for a loop.

"It's empty," Poblano said, beginning his scan of the room from behind the open door.

Along the far wall, a desk stood in front of an expansive multi-paned window over which the venetian blinds had been raised, allowing indirect sunlight into the room. The desk, typical of those assigned to professors, dominated the office with its mammoth-like bulk, but nothing appeared on it. No computer. No printer. No books or stacks of memos. It looked as unused as any piece of furniture sitting in a warehouse. Flanking it on both sides, two bookshelves stood along the walls. Rising nearly to the ceiling, they had enough capacity to hold hundreds of books, but they too were bare. Facing the desk stood two wooden armchairs. As if awaiting a pair of visitors, Robert thought. *Or accommodating two ghostly ones.*

A chill rippled up the young man's spine. "Are you sure this is the right office?"

"The key Davis gave me fit the lock," Poblano murmured.

Exchanging copies of keys was a special arrangement the professors had had. If LaCroix needed something from her office, Davis might pick it up for her, and vice versa. Both of them worked a lot from home.

Poblano ran a fingertip over the desktop. It came away clean, indicating that the desk could not have been unattended for very long. Someone had been using it—or at least dusting it.

"Maybe she recently moved to another office," Robert suggested. *But then why would her nameplate, still affixed to the door, have been left behind?*

Poblano pulled open a drawer to see if the desk was as empty inside as out. Meanwhile, the young man lingered at the entrance, wary of interfering with what was starting to look like an increasingly serious and complex undertaking. *A missing professor. An empty office. An abandoned nameplate. Maybe Davis was not as crazy as she seemed. Maybe...*

Sounds from down the hall arrested his thoughts. He turned to look.

Four or five offices away stood a tall, robust woman in olive-green pants and a white blouse. She appeared to be scolding a man in a drab, gray, janitorial shirt, baggy work trousers, and smudgy, white, gym shoes. He was clutching the handle of a mop, its head submerged inside a yellow plastic bucket on tiny wheels, absorbing the reprimand, his shaggy head bowed, while she towered over him, her impressive height enhanced by a pair of shiny, black pumps.

Robert strained to pick up what she was saying, but the echoey hallway distorted her words beyond recognition. Suddenly, like a lioness startled by the crackle of a footfall, she turned her eyes toward LaCroix's office, spotting Robert. He snapped his face away and, for several seconds, pretended not to hear the click of her high heels as she approached him over the tiled floor.

"You must be the police," she said, stopping a few feet away.

He turned, heart pounding. "Na... no, ma'am."

Her eyes—large, blue and fearless—were fixed on him.

"No, ma'am, we're not the police."

An incident flashed through his mind from years before when on a hike through Yellowstone National Park he encountered a rider on a horse. He had never seen a horse except on television. The animal's beauty, strength and size took him by surprise, leaving him breathless for a moment. Similarly astounded now, he confronted this bigger-than-life woman whose face, framed by her bountiful, blond coiffure, seemed to radiate not only superior intelligence but an all-engulfing, invincible vitality.

"That maintenance man over there..." she threw a curt sideways nod down the hall. "I told him more than once to use 'Wet Floor' signs when mopping the floor so that people won't slip and break their necks. I almost broke mine yesterday exiting the restroom! And why was he mopping here anyway? He's not supposed to be mopping in Wilkinson Hall on a Saturday morning!"

Poblano poked his head out of LaCroix's office.

"I'm Robyn Templeton," the woman turned immediately to him. "*Professor* Robyn Templeton. And you are?"

He fished an identity card out of his suitcoat. "Joseph Poblano, private investigator. And this is my assistant, Robert Connelly."

Robert bowed his head. The woman kept her eyes on Poblano. "You're not the police then?"

"No. Were you expecting the police?"

"Yes, and I'll tell you why. But would you mind stepping into my office? I'd prefer to explain things in a more private setting." She glanced down the hall again, but the custodian was now gone—or at least nowhere in sight.

Conveniently, Templeton's office lay just a few feet away, facing LaCroix's. It had the same layout: a heavy, wooden desk in front of a big multi-paned window with two armchairs facing the desk. The venetian blinds were closed and lowered against the sun's glare. She sat behind the desk while Poblano took a seat in one of the armchairs, Robert sitting to his right.

"When I saw you, I presumed a theft had been reported."

"You mean—"

She nodded. "Professor LaCroix's office appears to have been robbed."

"It appears to have been *cleared out.*"

"Indeed. Professor LaCroix contacted you?"

"No."

"Oh?"

"We're trying to locate her. She seems to have dropped

out of touch with everyone since yesterday evening. I thought we might find her here or at least a clue as to where she might be. I never expected to find her office vacated."

Templeton appeared perplexed. "Well, that's a surprise to *me*. Two surprises, in fact, one being that you didn't know about the vacated office and the other being that Ilona's missing."

"*Apparently* missing," Poblano corrected her.

"There's no question which one of those worries me more. I do hope she's all right."

"We have no reason to believe she isn't."

"Have you found her car?"

"Her car is at her apartment. She never used it Friday."

"What about her smartphone? You could track her by that, couldn't you?"

"She left it at home."

"Hmm…" Templeton thought a while. "Maybe she didn't *want* to be tracked."

"Could be," Poblano nodded thoughtfully. "We're considering all possibilities."

Templeton's eyes narrowed. "If not Ilona, then who contacted you?"

"I can't disclose that."

"Of course, of course," Templeton nodded quickly, as if eager to show that any impropriety was entirely unintended.

"Can you tell us how LaCroix's office was cleared out?"

"I'd be glad to. It happened yesterday afternoon around two. I was here at my desk when the clean-up crew arrived."

"Clean-up crew?"

"Let me explain. Dear old George, George Hamilton, passed away rather suddenly a week ago—a heart attack, I understand—and he left behind an office full of old books and journals and copies of research articles. With few exceptions none of them was wanted by anyone. Who wants more paper to lug around when the whole world is going digital?"

Poblano nodded, partly to show agreement, partly to nudge her on.

"So, the administration arranged to have his office cleared of all that 'paper junk.' They hired a clean-up crew to do the job on Friday afternoon. But when they arrived, they seemed confused about which office to clear out.

"The only explanation I can think of is that the two offices, Hamilton's and LaCroix's, lie next to each other, divided by the same wall. I suppose a stranger who couldn't read might ignore the nameplates and mistake one office for the other."

Poblano nodded.

"Still, it's hard to believe that such a mix-up could have occurred. Yet I suppose that stranger things have happened…"

"Who was the head of the clean-up crew?"

Templeton leaned back, consulting her memory. "Ah, yes, *Sánchez*. Ramón Sánchez. His English, although better than that of the two guys with him, was quite rudimentary. Therefore, I indicated Hamilton's office by pointing directly at it. How he could have misunderstood me, I have no idea."

"So, despite your attempt at clarification, he took LaCroix's office for Hamilton's?"

"Apparently, yes."

"And you couldn't correct the mistake later?"

"I was gone before they started. I left about five after two."

"To attend the conference?"

"The conference?"

"At the hotel."

"Oh, no," she shook her head, chuckling. "I attended Wednesday and Thursday, but none of the Friday panels interested me. And I had work to complete here."

Poblano jotted something down on a notepad then looked up again at the woman behind the desk. "So, you wouldn't have been here if Professor LaCroix returned in the evening?"

"Did she return?"

"We have reason to believe so."

"Who told you that?"

"Professor," Poblano cleared his throat, shifting a little in his chair. "My sources must remain confidential at least for now."

"Of course, of course." Templeton looked a bit flustered, but only briefly. "To answer the question, no, I would not have been here if Ilona returned. As I've said, shortly after Sánchez arrived, I went home. The work of his crew would have distracted me too much. I'm a very easily distracted person, detective." She flashed him a manufactured smile.

"I imagine that Professor LaCroix would have been shocked to find her office empty."

"She certainly would have been! Any professor would be. Her computer, printer, books, papers—all gone! I do hope she keeps copies of everything or at least everything she really needs. A loss like that, one of that magnitude, could set her research back months, even years."

"Is that so?"

"I'm quite sure of it. Ilona's researching ethnic tensions between peripheries and metropoles in predominantly Spanish-speaking countries, including Spain. She's a budding guru in this area. Have you heard of the separatist movement in Catalonia?"

"A little," Poblano lied.

"Ilona is investigating it. She is, how shall I put this… the envy of the department when it comes to the application of quantitative methods and linguistic abilities. Her Spanish, French, and Portuguese are superb, and she knows several dialects, including the main ones in Latin America."

"She must be highly gifted," Poblano said, anxious to steer the talk back to the investigation. "Where would Sánchez have taken her belongings?"

"Heaven knows. A landfill?"

"Do you think there's a chance we could recover them or at least some of them?"

"I have no idea."

"What's the name of that junk-hauling company?"

"I… I don't know. Sánchez and something, I'd guess."

Seeing Poblano rise from his chair, Robert rose too.

"Thank you, professor," Poblano said. "We appreciate your help."

Templeton stood up with a look of concern. "I do hope nothing's happened to Ilona."

"We share that hope."

"Has a missing-persons report been filed?"

"No."

"You will keep me informed, won't you, detective? That's what you are, isn't it, a detective?"

"A private investigator. Yes, we will keep you informed…" Poblano paused, "in accordance with your need to know. Thank you again, professor."

* * *

Just minutes after leaving Templeton's office, Robert was in the front passenger's seat of Poblano's 1996 Toyota Camry pecking madly away at his phone. "I found it!" he exclaimed. Although no one had faulted him for anything, he felt a surge of vindication, proud to show both his mentor and himself that he could help in the case.

A company founded by someone with the name Ramón Sánchez popped up on his screen: Trash Be Gone! "This must be it," the young man said. "How many Sánchez's can there be in the garbage-hauling business?"

"You'd be surprised," Poblano seemed to sigh and smirk at the same time.

Perplexed by the response, Robert looked at him.

"Hispanics are doing three-quarters of the work now. I mean the real work. The man's work. Construction. Warehouse. Auto-mechanics. Sanitation. Trucking. Landscaping. Ever see a Jew in landscaping? All the manly jobs are going to the Hispanics. Where is this place anyway, this Trash-Be-Gone place?"

Robert read off the address.

"Humboldt Park?"

"That's what it says here. You familiar with it?"

"Too familiar. It's crawling with spics."

Robert winced. Poblano put his foot to the accelerator. The Camry sped off.

Situated near the end of a strip mall was a Mexican grocery store with the name MERCADO over the entrance. Next to it, at the very end of the mall, was the address they were seeking, a plain, eggshell-white, one-story building, its nondescript front door facing the avenue underneath the sign "Trash Be Gone!"

Sitting behind a desk in the front office, if one could call it a front office, was a short, heavyset man of between 40 and 50 with a large, round face and the weatherbeaten look of one accustomed to working in the elements. He was dressed in a dark green T-shirt suitable for outdoor work, his black hair in a crewcut.

"May I help you?" he eyed the visitors, cautious, curious, the pencil in his stubby fingers frozen above a form he'd been filling out.

"*Sí, Señor*," Poblano came up to the desk, adding with a chuckle that this was all the Spanish he knew.

"It's all right, sir." The man gave a quick, cordial nod. "I can speak English if you like."

They touched fists, a gesture that, since the worst of the pandemic, had come to replace the custom of shaking hands.

"Pardon us for interrupting your morning." Poblano glanced at the yet-to-be-completed form.

The man shrugged, dismissing the need for an apology. "May I help you?"

"You are Ramón Sánchez?"

"Yes."

"Pleased to meet you. I'm Joseph Poblano, a private investigator." Poblano showed his identification card. "This is my assistant Robert Connelly."

A worried look flashed over the man's face.

"Nothing to worry about, Mr. Sánchez. We are not the police."

Poblano's "assurance" seemed to exacerbate the discomfort, Sánchez's anxiousness ratcheting up a notch at the mention of police.

"We're just gathering information concerning a trash

pick-up yesterday afternoon. You picked up trash at the university yesterday, is that right?"

"Yes, sir." Sánchez nodded, his nervous eyes shifting between Poblano and Robert.

"We have reason to believe that through no fault of your own, you may have removed items still valuable to their owner and still very much wanted by her. If possible, we'd like to recover those items."

"Items?"

"Books, magazines, computer, printer…"

"But…. but my men only removed what they were told to remove."

"I understand," Poblano nodded. "But there was a mistake. Not your fault. You were given the wrong directions, the wrong room."

"Wrong room?"

"Yes. This was not your fault. I have only one question now: Could those items be recovered?"

The proprietor's eyes acquired a distant look, as if he were running a train of technically problematic operations through his mind. "It may not be easy," he sighed. "All yesterday's pick-ups have been taken to landfills. We keep nothing for more than a few hours. We could not do business if we hung on to anything longer than that."

"What about the computer?" Robert asked, heart pounding, eager to show his usefulness. "Landfills don't typically take electronic junk." Looking to Poblano for confirmation, he received more than he expected: The detective was looking back at him admiringly, impressed by the young man's acuity.

Sánchez also turned to the young man. "That is true, sir,

but..." he shook his head regretfully. "What happens after those materials are received, how long they are held, where they are disposed of, I have no idea. It's not my business."

He gave the addresses of several disposal sites for electronic devices. "I'm not sure to which place the items were taken. I'd have to ask Pedro or Miguel."

"Are they here?" Poblano asked.

"They are off today. And tomorrow is Sunday. They'll be off tomorrow. In fact,..." Sánchez turned to a bulletin board on the wall behind the desk. "They're not scheduled to work again until Tuesday."

Poblano bit his lower lip. Robert could all but hear the wheels of his mentor's mind turning. Waiting until Tuesday was out of the question. They could ask Sánchez for Pedro and Miguel's addresses and phone numbers, but even if the boss divulged that information—and it was unclear he felt any obligation to do so—could the employees be located? Maybe they were doing what Poblano himself would be doing had it not been for the call from Marla Davis, enjoying a Saturday with their families. Quite possibly, they were at work at second jobs that had nothing to do with "Trash Be Gone!" (Whatever sins characterized Hispanics, sloth was not one of them.) But be they at home or at work, how would it look to barge in on them with questions about a trash-hauling incident from yesterday?

"Thank you for your help," was all Poblano said, ending the interview.

"I'm sorry I could not have helped more," Sánchez shrugged with that expression which always reminded Robert of a puppy caught pooping on the living room rug. "If you'd like to... to pursue this—"

The detective waved away the suggestion, turning toward the door.

The proprietor's voice sounded again, however, causing him to stop. "Will... will the university sue me?"

Poblano froze, taken aback for a moment. Slowly he turned to face the proprietor. "No," he said. "It wasn't your fault."

But as he followed his mentor out the door, Robert glanced again at the large, round, melon-like face behind the desk, seeing only anxiety there.

* * *

"I think we left him in doubt," the young man said.

Poblano nodded. "To tell you the truth, I don't know how the university handles situations like this and, frankly, I don't care. It's none of my business. I'm here to calm a frantic woman so that she can tell other women that I handled her concerns respectfully and effectively.

"That's how the world works, kid. Unlike in the classroom, out here you must focus on whatever you do for a living and avoid distractions. Otherwise, you'll be eaten alive. Davis is paying me to be here now. If she weren't, do you think I'd be sacrificing a Saturday with my wife and kids?"

They were sitting in Poblano's car, "Trash Be Gone!" still visible across the street. In front of them, cars and trucks whizzed by in both directions, oblivious of the nearly empty parking lot, the Camry parked in it, and the two men ruminating behind the dashboard.

Robert scanned the far side of the roadway, noting the MERCADO sign again. To the left of it ran a series of other businesses: an orthodontist's office, a restaurant, coffee shop, boutique, hardware store, a florist, all except the hardware store bearing Spanish names. Customers, many of them women with strollers or toddlers in tow, entered and exited the shops, suggesting a thriving commercial center.

The other side of the street, the side where he and Poblano were sitting, had a totally different look. A decrepit wooden fence divided the parking lot from a neighborhood of bleak, three-story, brick apartment buildings with passageways and courtyards that looked not only starved for sunlight but downright scary. Affixed to the back sides of the buildings were rickety-looking stairways made of wooden planks that, from a distance, resembled gray popsicle sticks glued together. As if braced for an assault, the buildings were fronted by black, wrought-iron fences designed to bar entry to all except the tenants.

The lot in which they were sitting had once supported a veterinarian's clinic, its name still posted in faded letters over the front door. Robert looked at the one-story building now stripped of its former identity. Every window had been smashed. Imagining the vandals, he pictured boys from the nearby apartments. *In a few years, they'd graduate to more lucrative activities. Peddling drugs. Selling firearms. Launching those crash-and-grab robberies one saw so often on the news nowadays.*

His gaze ended on a spoiled head of cauliflower lying in a heap of rotting vegetables at the base of the fence. Nearby, a white butterfly was fluttering above a dandelion.

"I don't trust her," Poblano murmured, talking to himself, apparently thinking of Templeton. "But I don't trust Sánchez, either." He was gazing out the windshield at nothing in particular.

"Why don't you trust Sánchez?"

"It's just a hunch I have—a feeling about what he might be involved in. You saw how he reacted when I mentioned the police?"

"You think he's crooked?"

"He might be, but even if he isn't, he probably knows crooks. He might know them without even knowing it," Poblano let out a bleak laugh.

"Why would you say that?"

"Well, for one thing..." The detective turned to the young man with a wry smile. "He's Latino."

Robert winced. "You wouldn't say that of an Italian, would you?"

"If the Italian's living in this neighborhood, I might."

"What if he's living in Wilmette?"

Poblano snorted. "This ain't Wilmette, kid. This whole area is turning into a Hispanic jungle, and it'll get worse when those migrants start flooding in." He referred to the ongoing influx of migrants bused up to Chicago mainly from Texas, most of them from Latin America.

"What does any of this have to do with Sánchez?" Robert asked.

Poblano stared calmly out the windshield. "These migrants aren't coming here for no reason."

"They want a better life. Isn't that why *our* forefathers came?"

"Our forefathers came legally. At least mine did. And they came so long ago that whatever impelled them would have no bearing on the case at hand."

Robert stared at him in disbelief. "You think that LaCroix's disappearance is connected to the migrant crisis?"

"It might be. Some of these migrants are coming from places where kidnapping is a widespread business, do you know that?"

The young man turned his eyes away.

"What I'm saying is that I'm beginning to think that we should consider the possibility that Marla Davis might not be totally nuts. Maybe something *has* happened to LaCroix."

"But this morning you thought that…"

"This morning was before I found out about Sánchez."

Robert's phone hummed and hummed again. "My father!" He pressed the phone to his ear. "Hi, Dad!"

"I just wanted to check up on you. Everything all right?"

"Yeah, yeah. Everything's fine."

"Is Detective Poblano teaching you anything?"

"A lot."

"Good. Pete recommended him, and I trust Pete."

Pete was an old friend of Robert's father and an old friend of Poblano's younger brother. Both in the business of selling medical equipment, neither Pete nor Robert's father knew much about private investigators, but his father liked Pete and Pete liked Poblano's brother, and that was all the basis they needed to recommend Poblano as a mentor.

"You'll be home for Mother's Day?"

"Of course, Dad."

"Maybe you can throw the old baseball around with Jenny's little boy." He mentioned Robert's sister who had a six-year-old son. "Your sisters are no good with stuff like that. Girls can't throw. We need a man around here."

"What's wrong with *you*, Dad?"

"I'm already committed."

"Committed to what?"

"Watching the Sox-Astros game on TV."

Robert laughed. "Look, I can't talk much right now. Believe it or not, I'm working."

"On a Saturday?"

"Yeah."

"Fine, fine. I'll say goodbye then. Be careful. We'll see you soon."

"Bye, Dad."

Robert rolled his eyes and turned back to Poblano. "Where were we? Oh, yes, you think that Davis might be on to something, that LaCroix might have been kidnapped, and that Sánchez might be in cahoots with her kidnappers?"

"Not necessarily in cahoots, just in association with. He probably knows a lot of Latinos, right? Maybe some illegals. Maybe some on the shady side. All I'm saying is, he might have bumped into some bad guys even without knowing it.

"Look at it from a crook's point of view. If kidnapping for ransom was my thing, and I knew someone who made a living removing junk from places that might be linked to money, I'd smell opportunities."

"You think professors make lots of money?"

"Some do."

Robert nodded. *This was true. A professor doing research in chemistry might make a mint in, say, the pharmaceutical industry.* "But LaCroix is in political science. You think poly-sci professors are millionaires?"

Poblano smirked. "Do you think crooks necessarily distinguish between one academic discipline and another? When a thug sees a professor, he sees privilege. He sees upper-class status. He smells money."

Poblano had a point. "So, you think that looking into

Sánchez's connections is the best use of our time?"

"It wouldn't be a waste of time. I'd start with his employees. Are they documented? Where do they come from? How long have they been here?"

Robert groaned inwardly, struck by the amount of time such an investigation might require. "But if LaCroix might have been kidnapped, shouldn't we notify the police right away?"

"CPD is overburdened." Poblano referred to the Chicago Police Department. "They won't act on a missing-persons case until we can present evidence that she's really missing. We're not even close to that."

"So, what now? Make a list of Sanchez's employees?"

"There's something we should do first."

Robert looked at him.

Poblano was rubbing his chin. "There must be security cameras at that school. A video might show what happened Friday afternoon in front of Templeton's office and, later, when LaCroix showed up."

"*If* she showed up, you mean."

Poblano nodded. "*If* she showed up."

SATURDAY AFTERNOON: CLOSING IN ON THE CULPRITS

Given the costly consequences of clearing out the wrong office as well as the mystery of LaCroix's disappearance, campus security was more than willing to cooperate. By 2:20 p.m., Robert and Poblano were in the basement of Chester Hall, reviewing relevant film footage.

"There she is," Poblano pointed at the computer screen.

Although somewhat grainy, the video showed a tall, blond woman in high heels emerge from Templeton's office shortly before two p.m. on Friday. "That's Templeton," Poblano murmured, his eyes glued to the screen.

Facing her in the hallway stood a short, chubby Hispanic man with a round face. "Sánchez."

To his left, just inside the screen, two Hispanic men were standing in black, rugged, steel-toed boots. "Pedro and Miguel," Poblano said. They appeared to be watching Sánchez and Templeton, awaiting instructions from their boss.

The exchange was brief. Templeton said something to Sánchez, returned to her office and, half a minute later, appeared in the hall again, closing and locking her door. She promptly departed, heading toward the stairwell and outside the scope of the camera.

"She lied," Robert said.

"What do you mean?" Poblano kept his eyes on the screen, unperturbed.

"She never pointed at Hamilton's door."

"She never pointed at LaCroix's either. So what?"

"So, she lied."

Poblano paused the video, still looking at the screen. "You know, people sometimes say things under stress that... that don't exactly comport with reality. That doesn't necessarily discredit them in my book."

Robert looked at his mentor, dubious. Poblano's explanation had a strained quality to it, as if he were going out of his way to spare Templeton an accusation that he would all too quickly have leveled at Sánchez.

"Our interview might have stressed her a little," the detective went on, "don't you think? Not stressed her *out* necessarily but put her under some pressure. To protect herself, she might have exaggerated a little, saying she pointed when she only spoke."

"She didn't strike me as the type who gets rattled easily."

"No, she's probably not. On the other hand, appearances can be deceptive."

With this glib generality, Poblano restarted the video. "You'd think that after Sánchez began clearing out the wrong office, someone might have come along and corrected his mistake."

"You'd think so," Robert agreed. The screen, however, showed nothing happening in the hallway while the office in question, off-screen, was being emptied. "The other profs were probably at that conference," the young man noted. "All of them except Templeton. And don't you find *that* a little odd—that she'd be the only one *not* at the conference?"

"I wouldn't hang too much on that."

An unexpected figure appeared on the screen. "I've seen

that guy," Robert said. "He's the maintenance man. I saw him this morning talking with Templeton."

"When did you see that?"

"While you were inside LaCroix's office."

The screen showed the custodian in the same baggy pants and gray shirt he'd worn that morning, pushing the same yellow bucket in front of him and stopping to gaze inside the office that Sánchez's workers were supposedly clearing out. "Yeah, that's definitely him!" Robert squinted at the grainy footage.

Sánchez appeared in the hallway again, having come out of the office where his men were at work. He and the maintenance man exchanged words.

"Too bad we don't have audio," Poblano murmured.

The verbal exchange appeared amiable. Toward the end, the maintenance man apparently said something funny. The men laughed and high-fived each other.

Poblano chuckled. "Workers of the world unite!"

Within seconds, they parted, the custodian disappearing off-screen to the left, Sánchez disappearing beneath the screen, rejoining his crew. Later, the screen showed him and his workmen carrying boxes into the hallway, heading for the stairwell.

"They work fast," Poblano murmured. "It took 'em just fourteen minutes to empty that office."

He depressed a button on the keyboard, fast-forwarding the video. More than four hours raced by in minutes, a grayish blur. At 7:10, he slowed down, inching forward from there. 7:15. 7:20. At 7:22 and ten seconds, the screen showed a woman of about 30 dressed in a business skirt and high heels, a handbag slung over her shoulder. She was nearing the top of the stairway.

"That's her," Poblano said. "That's LaCroix."

She entered the same area where Sánchez and Templeton had stood hours before, removed a key from her handbag, and inserted it into the door. She pushed open the door and, although what she saw lay beyond the scope of the camera, some of her reaction to it was caught on film. She stopped or, more precisely, froze. "She's seeing it now," Poblano murmured, "the empty office."

With little more than the top of her head visible, Robert could only imagine her jaw dropping. *Like that of someone near the top of a skyscraper about to enter an elevator only to find the elevator's floor missing, having dropped down several dozen stories.* He could all but hear the gasp.

Unfrozen, as it were, she whipped around, turning away from her office. "She's put two and two together," Poblano said. "She knew that Hamilton's office was to be cleared out. She's figured there'd been a mix-up."

Surprisingly, though, she turned toward the south end of the hall, not the way she'd come up. Then she took off at a run.

"Why that way?" Poblano murmured to himself.

"She wanted to catch up with whoever took her belongings?" Robert suggested.

"But why in that direction?"

Poblano jotted down the time on his notepad. "7:23." He thought for a moment then turned to Robert. "Here's what I think. Someone knew in advance about this dead guy's office needing to be cleared out, probably someone who knows Sánchez and his junk-removal business, and he exploited the situation. Bad guys were waiting downstairs for LaCroix. She noticed them on her way in and something about them made her want to avoid them on her way out. That's why she went the other way, toward the south staircase.

"But she really had no escape. They were waiting for her at either end. They knew she'd be shocked and desperate to recover her things. Posing as the clean-up crew, they invited her to their vehicle where supposedly she could retrieve her lost items. As a result, she went with them, unresisting, even with a sense of relief, perhaps even thanking them, only to be shoved into their vehicle and driven away."

Robert ran the theory through his mind. "It's a little convoluted, don't you think? I mean, if you're the kidnappers, why bother with emptying her office, having it emptied, or waiting for it to be emptied? Why not just grab her?"

Poblano shrugged. "Maybe these crooks are unusually sophisticated. Some bugs just eat other bugs. But there are bugs that anaesthetize their prey before ingesting."

Robert frowned. "But how would they have known that LaCroix was returning to her office Friday evening?"

"Maybe they *didn't* know. Maybe they just waited, hoping she'd appear, and they got lucky."

Robert frowned again. Too many "maybe's" for his taste. "If this is all true, then shouldn't there be a ransom note coming?"

"Maybe there's already been one."

Robert looked at Poblano. "To whom?"

"Her grandfather."

"She has a grandfather?"

"Jacques LaCroix. He lives in Green Bay. He's the one who raised her after her parents were killed. He's about all the family she's had since then."

"Davis told you this?"

Poblano nodded.

Robert shook his head, stunned. "Poor girl. I mean, even if she hasn't been kidnapped, even if she's perfectly okay, to have grown up like that!"

"Listen, let's not get lost here. Remember what we're doing: trying to find a missing person."

"Right, right," Robert nodded, as if snapping out of a reverie—or a bad dream.

"Davis gave me the grandfather's number," Poblano tapped it out on his phone. A pause followed. Robert and his mentor exchanged glances.

"Is this Jacques LaCroix? Glad to hear you, sir… No, I'm not here to announce you've won the lottery!" the detective chuckled. "No, nothing like that. I'm Detective Joseph Poblano, private investigator." A pause followed. "No, no, sir. Nothing bad has happened.

"I was contacted by a friend of your granddaughter's, a Professor Marla Davis. Do you know her? Yes, from the university… She's the one, yes. A very nice lady, yes… I agree. She's concerned over being unable to reach Ilona since yesterday evening.

"Yes, that's right… They were at the conference here in Chicago and… You say that Ilona often likes to drop out of touch for a day or two? She's been doing that since high school? But… but her friend, Professor Davis, is concerned and…

"No, I'm not the police… Just a private… yes, a *private* investigator. Yes, that's right. This is a kind of wellness check. Your granddaughter may turn up at any time, you say? Probably will?

"You haven't heard anything, then, is that right?" Poblano nodded. "You'll contact me if you hear anything?" He recited his phone number.

"Good. That's great. And we'll call you too… as soon as we learn something.

"Oh, and just one more thing. Do you know anyone besides yourself who might know anything about Ilona's whereabouts?"

Robert heard a voice coming through the phone, sounding irritable now, the words unintelligible.

"Bachmann? Daniel Bachmann? Can you spell that please? B A C H M A N… A double N? Let me write that down."

Poblano set the phone on the desk and hastily jotted down a name and address. He repeated it over the phone. "Yes, I got it. Thank you, Mr. LaCroix. Thank you, sir. Goodbye for now."

Robert stared at his mentor. "Well?"

"Well," Poblano wetted his lips, "it appears that our missing professor has a boyfriend—or *had* one. A Mr. Daniel Bachmann with whom she recently broke up after a nasty fight. This looks promising."

* * *

The Toyota Camry pulled into a parking space across the street from the Bachmann house, not far north of the Plaza Del Lago in one of Chicago's wealthiest suburbs. "Why do they call this Kenilworth?" Poblano withdrew the key from the ignition. "It surely ain't no kennel!"

Robert responded with a wan smile. "I didn't know you were so clever with words, sir."

In truth, even the doghouses in this lakefront suburb

sixteen miles north of the city looked attractive. Residences lining the streets and those further north in Winnetka consisted mainly of big, three-story homes of brick or stone standing amid magnificent pines, poplars, and elms, some of the trees over a century old, their branches now cloaked in the translucent green foliage of early May. Driveways led over lawns of lush, tender, spring grass from the pretty streets to spacious backyards with swimming pools, fire pits, rock gardens and greenhouses. A goldfinch spurted across Robert's field of vision, darting from one tree into the leafy canopy of another, as if reveling in the sheer delight of being alive.

"Is this the Bachmann house?" Poblano asked when a woman in a hot-pink spandex running suit answered the door.

She looked to be in her late thirties but might well be a decade and a half older, Robert thought. *Appearances belonged to the quality of life, and these North Shore women had ways of keeping up appearances.* He thought of the millions of dollars of vitamins, dietary supplements, exercise regimens, clothes and cosmetics, not to mention annual trips to Florida to escape Chicago's winters, which went into "quality of life."

In her pink running outfit, she cast hard eyes on the visitors. "You're not Jehovah's Witnesses, are you?"

"No, ma'am," Poblano said.

"Mormons?"

The detective chuckled. "Do we look like preachers of the Word?" he smiled at Robert. "No, ma'am, we're not evangelizers of any kind."

"Then you must be delivering a package. Do you have my package?"

"Package?"

"The new running shoes I ordered from Amazon?"

Robert looked down at her current running shoes. They were gleaming white. *How did women do that, keeping even their running shoes immaculate?* This woman probably had several pairs.

"I'm Joseph Poblano, private detective, and this is my assistant Robert Connelly."

The woman looked disappointed. "I've been waiting forever for those shoes. It's been over two days now since I ordered them. And I've got Amazon Prime!"

She sounded outraged. "Amazon Prime" was a special arrangement for speedier delivery. Subscribers paid extra for the privilege.

"You're private investigators?"

"Yes."

One could sense her defenses go up, much as Sánchez's had.

"We're looking into something with which your son might be able to help."

"My son?"

"Daniel."

"What's this about?"

"Do you know a Professor LaCroix? Ilona LaCroix?"

"Oh…" Her voice spun downward like a piece of shrapnel off a doomed rocket.

"We're trying to locate her. A friend of hers hasn't been able to reach her since yesterday evening and she's grown concerned that—"

"I don't want any more to do with that person. I thought she was out of our lives and now… Here she is again!" Mrs. Bachmann heaved a sigh of frustration. "Look, I don't have time for this. I've got to get to my appointment at the fitness center. You couldn't come back another day, could you?"

"If you please, ma'am, I would not wish to delay."

The woman was shaking her head, expressing some combination of disbelief, disgust, and weariness.

"We'll keep it brief. Is Daniel home?"

"He's busy, studying for exams."

"I promise, this won't take more than a few minutes."

Surprising both his mother and her visitors, Daniel appeared from some interior region of the house, thumping into the vestibule in his stocking feet, anxious to see who was at the door. Seeing only Robert and Poblano, he seemed to deflate instantly, like a zeppelin collapsing on a football field. But only for a moment. Stung by the discourtesy his display of disappointment might have implied, he rushed to make amends.

"Who are these gentlemen, Mother?" he smiled at the visitors.

In short pants and a T-shirt, nearly a foot taller than his mother, Daniel Bachmann had a ruggedly handsome face with a thick, dark, curly head of hair, chocolate-brown eyes, and broad shoulders that suggested he might be or could have been a serious athlete.

"Honey…" his mother eyed Robert and Poblano with a smirk. "These men are private investigators. They'd like to ask you a few questions about…" she lowered her voice, "Jezebel."

"Ilona?" His eyes lit up. "Is she…" he turned to Poblano, "in some kind of trouble?"

The detective looked left then right, as if a neighbor might be eavesdropping. "Do you mind if we come in?"

The Bachmanns responded, their overlapping voices in

cacophony, the mother objecting, the son welcoming. "Please come in," Daniel overrode his mother, eclipsing her frown with a smile as he ushered the visitors into the breakfast room.

"Would you like anything? A cup of iced tea maybe? Coffee? I've been drinking lots of coffee lately."

"No, thanks," Poblano pulled a chair out from under the table. "I promised we'd be brief and we will."

Robert noticed the mother lingering nearby, watching from the kitchen. "I'm studying for comprehensive exams," Daniel remarked.

"Oh?" Robert replied, genuinely curious. "What's your discipline?"

"Toxicology."

"I was in sociology. Three years. A doctoral program. I quit. Are you working on a doctorate?"

"I am. Why'd you leave sociology?"

"I couldn't see any future in it. For myself, I mean."

Daniel bobbed his head in the way people do when wishing to show interest but unsure how to respond.

"You study poisons?" Poblano asked.

"You might say that." Daniel chuckled. "I'm doing my dissertation on neurotoxins, focusing on a toxin produced in certain fish, including the pufferfish. Ever hear of that fish?"

Poblano shook his head.

"The toxin I'm researching is also produced in several other animals, for example, some octopuses, newts, and snails as well as in certain bacteria. It kills by blocking messages sent through the nervous system, paralyzing the victim and leading to respiratory distress."

He went galloping on, lost in his own enthusiasm, unwittingly showering his guests with esoteric scientific terms and arcane empirical references. Poblano cleared his throat. "That's all quite fascinating, but… May we ask a few questions about Ilona?"

Daniel was embarrassed. "Sorry. I get carried away." His enthusiasm completely gone, he looked suddenly serious.

"When was the last time you saw her?" Poblano asked.

"Sunday. Sunday morning of last week. We had a long talk at her place. She lives in an apartment near campus. I'm afraid I became rather angry."

"What about?"

"Oh… our future. I'd been dating Ilona for over two years. I hoped to marry her someday. She knew that."

"You bet she did," his mother said.

"She's such a beautiful woman!" A dreamy look came into the young man's eyes. "When I first met her, I could hardly believe a woman like her would go with me."

His mother released a muffled snort.

"So, what led to the argument?" Poblano inquired, his voice unusually gentle, empathetic.

"Look, detective, I'm almost thirty. Ilona's almost thirty-three. I wanted to start building a family. Unfortunately, she… she had other plans."

"Other plans?"

"Like pursuing her academic career. She was hooked on that career. And you know, in a way, I can understand that. She'd spent six and a half years earning a doctorate and another three years working as an assistant professor, and now here she was, coming up for tenure. And she was working on this big research project funded by the National Science Foundation. She needed to publish.

"She had no time for children. That was the upshot. She

said it might be three or four more years before she could even *consider* having a child. She started talking about having her eggs frozen and, maybe, using a surrogate, and... Well, that's what did it for me. I'd had enough.

"I wanted nothing to do with *in vitro* fertilization. I wanted children the old-fashioned way, and I wanted them while my spouse and I were both still young enough to be real parents. So, I... I quit the relationship."

"Good riddance!" his mother harrumphed.

"You got angry with her?" Poblano asked, keeping his eyes on Daniel.

"Yes," the young man looked remorseful. "Yes, I'm afraid I did."

"Did you... get rough with her?"

"Rough?"

"Did you hit her?"

"Oh, no! Nothing like that. I would never do that. But I stomped out of her place. I vowed never to see her again. It was an ugly scene. For both of us, I think."

"She misled him," Mrs. Bachmann said. "She stole valuable years of my son's life."

"It wasn't like that at all!" Daniel closed his eyes. "We were so deeply in love. Last year, she converted to Judaism for me."

"Really?"

Daniel nodded, eyes still closed.

"Do you have any idea where she might be right now?"

"I don't know," the young man whispered, shaking his head.

Poblano watched him closely, his investigator's antennae quivering, straining to catch any detail, any fine point the subject might be omitting.

"I don't know," Daniel repeated, opening his eyes. "I...
I hope she hasn't done anything to... to hurt herself." He
turned to Poblano with a look of alarm.

"We share your sentiments," Poblano stood up.

The meeting ended. The detective thanked Daniel for his
cooperation. Robert wished him well in his research. After
promising to keep him informed about Ilona, they bowed to
his mother, who gladly escorted them back to the front door
and out of her house.

* * *

"What do you think?" Robert asked when they were comfort-
ably seated again behind the dashboard of the Camry.

"I think we better pull out of here before she calls the
police," Poblano joked. Putting his foot to the accelerator, he
headed for a nearby restaurant in downtown Wilmette. "Do
you like Thai food?"

"Fine with me."

Robert ordered stir-fried Thai basil and pork while Poblano
went for the green curry with chicken and eggplant, and they
both had hot and sour shrimp soup. "I couldn't pronounce
this if my life depended on it," Poblano stared at the menu.
Gaeng Keow Wan Gai. "I can eat it, but I can't pronounce it."

"Do you like Thai cuisine?" Robert raised a spoonful of
the spicy soup to his lips.

"I like almost any kind of cuisine unless it has insects in it,
you know, grasshoppers, nightcrawlers—that sort of thing."

"I agree with you there, although I've heard insects can be
an excellent source of protein."

"For anteaters maybe. I'll eat almost anything, though,

when I'm hungry. That's why I married Gloria. She's a great cook and I love to eat. A match made in heaven! What were your impressions of Bachmann?"

"Him or his mother?"

"Him."

"Well…" Robert wiped his mouth on a napkin, searching for just the right words.

"He seems to have the know-how," Poblano went on. "Enough knowledge and enough intelligence to figure out how to do something really cunning. A smart guy."

"You think he'd hurt LaCroix?"

"Step back and look at the big picture, kid. Pretend you're one of the gods on Mount Olympus. From there, you see three reasons why mortals do ugly things."

"You mean ugly things like kidnapping?"

"Kidnapping, murder, robbing, tormenting, you name it."

"What are the three reasons?"

"Money, sex, and revenge. That's it. I challenge you to find another."

Robert considered the proposition then nodded, accepting the premise. "Okay. Go on," he leaned over the table for another spoonful of soup.

"He doesn't appear to need money, but he's clearly lost access to a very beautiful woman."

"Sex?"

Poblano nodded. "Did you notice that picture of her on the wall in the breakfast room?"

"I did. I'm amazed it escaped his mother's attention."

"Oh, I'm sure it didn't. She'd probably incinerate it in an instant if he allowed her to sink her talons into it. But he won't. That's just my point. He's clinging to what he's lost. He resents the loss. It could be making his blood boil, and when a man's blood boils…"

Robert pictured the photo again. It might have been taken last spring then magnified on paper to be framed and proudly hung on a wall. It showed LaCroix in the sort of gown a woman might don for a formal party or an evening at the opera—a midi dress with flutter shoulders, dark red, lustrous, wrapped around her figure to reveal a hint of cleavage in her comely bust while accentuating the curves of her hips. She was standing, posing in front of Buckingham Fountain with the Chicago skyline behind her, perfectly at ease in the dress, looking at the cameraman with a playfully seductive smile, obviously having a blast.

She had a French look, Robert thought, recalling her light complexion, nose, lips, and the color of her hair (strawberry-blond), hair done up in a coiffure that seemed to bounce on her shoulders. Cheerful. Free-spirited. Nonchalant. Yet there was something else about her too, something in the eyes, those dark, Kalamata-olive eyes, that suggested ancestral strains stemming less from the Île-de-France than from the Mediterranean, an underlying sultry sadness that whispered more of the Peloponnese than of Normandy, Brittany, Strasbourg or Paris.

"She's too good-looking to be a professor," Poblano mumbled, speaking around a mouthful of brown rice.

"Probably too nice too," Robert murmured.

"What's that?"

"She's probably too nice to be a professor."

"Well…" Poblano swallowed some tea to wash down the rice, "we don't know that."

"So, you think Bachmann might be harboring a nefarious motive, something to do with sex?"

Poblano shoved his spoon into a pile of rice. "What do you think? Did you get a look at the size of the backyard?"

"What do you mean?"

"She could be lying six feet under right now, inside that backyard, traces of some neurotoxin still in her."

Robert frowned, repulsed by the thought. "No, no," he shook his head, "I don't think so. I think you've got it all wrong. I don't care about means, motive, or opportunity, or if he was offered a hundred million dollars to do something that awful. He just wouldn't do it."

"You sure?" Poblano lifted a hot pepper off the side of his dish to examine it before sampling it.

"Yeah, I'm sure, and here's why: The affect is all wrong. Bachmann didn't show any of the nervousness of a normal person who had just committed an atrocity, nor did he display the cool indifference of a psychopath."

Poblano nodded thoughtfully. "Wow, this is hot!" He set aside the pepper minus the tiny bite he had taken, smacking his lips. "Very good. Sometimes, you have to listen to your intuition, don't you? Facts are important, but they're not everything. No matter what the Catholic Church may say, right reason and good intentions aren't everything. Emotion matters. Passions count. Feelings are the stuff of life. If someone shows the wrong feelings or fails to show the right ones—that's a red flag."

Poblano daubed his lips with his napkin, took a sip of tea, and looked up at Robert, blinking away the tears that had sprung into his eyes upon biting into the hot pepper. "You're making progress, kid. I'm proud of you. So, where would we go from here?"

"I'd go back to Templeton. There was something about her

that bothered me. Her demeanor. Temperament. Attitude. And she lied! I still say she lied! She never pointed to Hamilton's office. And what she said about Sánchez was a lie too. His English isn't half bad."

"Hold your horses!" Poblano raised his hand. "What motive would Templeton have to direct Sánchez to clear out the wrong office?"

Robert shook his head, staring blankly at the table. "I don't know. But..." he looked up with sudden conviction, "maybe we should look into it."

Poblano shook his head discouragingly. "We'd be wasting our time. Let me tell you something. Lots of people have motives to commit crimes. Most, I would say. How many people have you known who've never been hard up for money? Never been spurned? Never felt themselves wronged, passed over, or stepped upon?"

Robert waited, his eyes fixed on his mentor.

"Everyone has criminal motives. You do. I do. The Pope does. But here's the remarkable thing: Very few of us ever commit crimes, I mean serious crimes. Felonies.

"We could infer some foul motive for Templeton—I'm sure we could find at least one—but so what? We can't show she did anything. There's no audio to that video. You say she failed to point to Hamilton's office. She'll say she misremembered. You say she told Sánchez to clear out the wrong office. She'll just deny it. It would be her word against his. Now, to muddy the picture—"

"It isn't muddy enough?" Robert chuckled.

"Grandfather Jacques says Davis is overreacting. He says his dear, sweet Ilona has a history of disappearing for a day or two without telling anyone. He's taking this in stride."

Robert sighed in frustration. "Why not just wait a day or two and see what happens?"

"Because I've been hired to investigate, so I feel I should at least pretend to be doing that. I can't afford to work for nothing, but I won't accept remuneration for nothing, either. Tomorrow's a Sunday. Do you go to church?"

"On Christmas and Easter."

"Good. I do too. We'll meet tomorrow then. Eight-thirty in the morning. I want to learn more about who comes and goes at this 'Trash Be Gone' place."

"Won't it be closed on a Sunday?"

"It probably will be. They're Mexicans. They'll be in church. The good ones will be. But remember," he winked, "we're not interested in the good ones."

SATURDAY EVENING:
A CLANDESTINE CALL

"For heaven's sake, Josh, *pick up!*" Robert addressed his old college buddy, venting annoyance into the phone. A couple hours had passed since Poblano had dropped him off near Bryn Mawr street. He was standing now by the window inside his studio apartment overlooking Sheridan Road, watching the traffic seven floors below.

It was flowing in both directions at its usual pace. Soon dusk would thicken and headlights would turn on, transforming motor vehicles into strings of luminescent pearls streaming through the streets of the Windy City.

He had called his old friend six times in the past ten minutes, obtaining only a recorded message. "This is Josh. Sorry. Can't answer right now. Please leave your message and I'll get back with you when I can."

When he could! Robert gave the red spot on the phone an angry tap, ending the attempted call. The one time in the past year that he most wanted his friend, Josh failed to answer.

One could never tell with Josh. Had he moved to New Zealand for work? Withdrawn into seclusion? Met a kindred spirit on the internet and taken off with her—or him—on a road trip à la Jack Kerouac? Or was he just lying on his bed listening to Taylor Swift, Doja Cat, or Ariana Grande? (Josh was obsessed with female singers.)

They had met in the first semester of graduate school,

embarking on the same doctoral program in sociology. On the cusp of taking his comprehensive exams, Robert withdrew, cutting his losses, as he saw it. But Josh persisted, claiming that he owed it to his father to obtain a Ph.D. degree. He obtained it in the usual time, about six years, then proceeded over the next year to send out over a hundred job applications to colleges and universities throughout the United States. The doors slammed in his face.

Meanwhile, his female colleagues, some of whom had yet even to obtain their degrees, enjoyed their choice of academic jobs. Good jobs, too. Tenure-track jobs. Jobs on which a career could be nurtured. Not the crappy, adjunct-professor positions the schools were throwing out like stale crumbs to the growing multitudes of starving job candidates. The explanation? Across the nation, colleges and universities needed to hire more women and persons of color because the Office of Civil Rights was holding a terrifying threat over their heads: Either meet the government's diversity, equity, and inclusion goals or lose your federal funding.

"Look," Josh once confided in a particularly heated moment. "We've had Karl Marx, Max Weber, Émile Durkheim, and Alexis de Tocqueville. We've even had Talcott Parsons. We don't need another white male sociologist!"

One of his two white male grandfathers, the one who had survived Auschwitz, emigrated to America at the age of 15, and had a successful career as a physician in Chicago, couldn't understand why his grandson was having such a hard time finding a job. "America is the land of opportunity!" he said. "What can't my grandson find work?"

One time, at two in the morning, Josh threatened to change his gender. "Why not?" he exclaimed over the phone.

"I've tried everything else!"

"Keep it down, Josh!" Robert whispered. "You'll wake up your parents."

"As a trans woman, I'd have my cake and eat it too. I'd have the brains of a white male Doctor of Philosophy and at the same time the status of an anointed minority."

Josh could sound a bit crazy at times.

But who could blame him? He had invested seven years of his life, played by the rules, passed through all the hoops, and now found himself with a sixty-thousand-dollar student-loan debt and unemployable. "That's right," he stressed, "not just unemployed but *unemployable*."

He recounted how some employers rejected him as over-qualified on account of his Ph.D. degree, while others considered him *improperly* qualified, his doctorate being in a field unrelated to the job, never mind that he had the brains to learn any job for which he applied. "I'd be better off with just a high school diploma," he once said.

He was probably right regarding some lines of work. Doors that might have opened to a 22-year-old college grad, were now shut in the face of a 34-year-old Doctor of Philosophy, forcing him to move back in with his parents.

"Look," he said, "My degree may say I'm a scholar, but I'm no martyr. If the choice is between sleeping on a subway vent in January and sleeping in my old bed, I'll take the bed."

"May I help you?" he answered the phone at last.

"Josh!"

"Big Bob?"

"It's the Big Bobber, yeah."

"Holy Cow! I must have accidentally erased your number. Anway, guess what? I got a job!"

"Fantastic!"

"At Jewel Osco—putting fruits and vegetables on the tables."

"Well…" Robert tried to sound encouraging, "it's *something!*"

"Yeah, it's something. Gets me out of the basement. And if I'm still working there in a year and a half, I'll qualify for health insurance. Union contract. What have you been up to lately?"

"I'm working as a private investigator."

"No! You serious?"

"Since the start of this month. I'm just a trainee really."

"So, you decided to pursue that criminology stuff?"

"I did."

"How much longer before you're in business for yourself?"

"Three years. I need three years of experience working with a PI to qualify for a license."

"You need a license for that?"

"In Illinois you do."

"How's it going?"

"Well, I'm into my first real case, and it's turning out to be more exciting than I thought. It might involve a…" Robert paused. "Look, I don't think I should say much about it. It's ongoing."

"You know something?" Josh cut in, "I think I should have gone into criminology. I feel I know it already, watching all those crime shows on TV." He stopped. A silence followed. "You still there, Bob?"

"Yeah, yeah. I'm still here."

"You went dead for a while. Anything the matter?"

"Listen, Josh, I was wondering if you could do me a favor.

I'm in a kind of dilemma, and it's regarding this case I've mentioned, the one I'm helping to investigate."

"Yeah? What's the dilemma?"

"It might be nothing, but then again… Look, I'd like to learn more about a certain professor at our alma mater, but my mentor has other ideas, and I have to stick mainly with him. I'm just the trainee. So, I was wondering if you could, maybe in an undercover sort of way, get some information for me."

"Oh, boy, maybe I *am* going into criminology!"

"Find out the status or circumstances of this professor I have in mind. Does she have tenure? If not, is she trying to obtain it? If so, what are her chances? Is she competing with anyone? Stuff like that, you know?"

"Big Bob, I have to level with you. I haven't been back at that viper's nest since I graduated. Outside sociology, I'd know hardly anyone anymore, and the ones I do know, the ones *inside* sociology, I'd probably want to avoid. And they'd probably want to avoid *me*."

"Do you remember a Professor Ilona LaCroix?"

A thoughtful pause followed. "History?"

"Political science."

"No, I can't say the name rings a bell."

"Maybe she arrived after you graduated. What about Robyn Templeton?"

"Was she the one with her nose in the air all the time, trotting about in nylons and high heels?"

Robert laughed. "I think you just nailed her."

"I couldn't approach somebody like that. I wouldn't even want her to remember me, and she probably wouldn't. I think I took one class of hers, 'House Congressional Voting' or something equally dull. I was one student in five hundred. It was a cattle course."

"Well, I've got good news for you. You wouldn't need to talk with her. In fact, I wouldn't want you to. Remember Maryanne McClosky, the head secretary in the dean's office?"

"That fat lady?"

"Yes!"

"She always reminded me of a giant beachball. Sure, I remember her. She was probably there two decades before we enrolled."

"I believe she's still there."

"Amazing."

"Her name's still listed on the school's website. Apparently, she's still the head secretary at the College of Liberal Arts."

"My God, she must have weighed 300 pounds!"

"She knew a lot about a lot of people, though. And, as I recall, she had a rather loose tongue."

"Did she ever! I learned more about the workings of the sociology department listening to her chatter than I could possibly have learned by any other means."

"That's my point. I was wondering if you could contact her, perhaps even this evening, and see if you could go out to lunch with her tomorrow."

A long pause followed in which Robert waited, biting his lip, half expecting his friend to break into bellowing laughter. But that's not what happened.

"I see your idea," Josh replied, sounding pensive, as if he were weighing the pros and cons.

"You don't find the idea totally nuts?"

"No, not at all. Maybe that's because crazy to crazy seems sensible."

"Could be. You doing anything Sunday?"

"No. It's one of my days off. I'm just part-time. How much are you paying?"

"I'll give you everything I earn from this case."

"Which is?"

"I don't know yet."

A brief pause followed. "You mean, you're assisting in an investigation and you have yet to inquire what you'll be paid?"

"Josh," Robert sighed, "imagine my situation. I don't want to come across as…"

"As what? Interested in your own survival?"

"No, it's not that. It's just that this is my first case and—"

"Bobby boy, haven't you wised up yet? That's how we were treated in grad school. They exploited us for our cheap labor, paid us peanuts, treated us with contempt, and left us high and dry. You don't have to put up with this!"

Robert held the phone away from his ear while Josh ranted on. When his friend began to run out of steam, he returned the phone to his ear. "I get where you're coming from but I really want this to succeed. *I* want to succeed. I'm trying to be careful not to make a bad impression."

"It's your life, Bob."

"Here's my idea. You could pose as a freelance writer doing a story on the school and its 'illustrious' political science department. That wouldn't be much of a lie. You are sort of a writer, aren't you?"

"Are you trying to insult me, Bob?"

"While visiting Chicago, you thought you'd take the opportunity to gather information about the department. You're living in Winnetka, right?"

"At my parents' house."

"So, you wouldn't have to lie there, either. You really *would* be visiting Chicago."

"But…"

"Hear me out. You send McCloskey an email tonight, explaining your request. Sunday's the only day you'll have to research this 'story' or whatever you're working on. You have to return to your day job Monday."

"That's true, by the way."

"Wonderful! You won't have to lie there, either."

"But here's the thing: Do you think she'd agree to go out to lunch with a guy she doesn't even know?"

"But she *does* know you! That's the beauty of it."

"She knows me?"

"McClosky had a photographic memory for names and faces. I'm sure she'd remember the guy with the Leon Trotsky look standing at the top of the marble staircase leading to Newton Hall. Remember? You were exhorting your fellow Americans to rise up against the war in Afghanistan?"

"Oh, brother!" Josh sounded embarrassed. "You think she'd remember *that*? I was just a freshman in undergrad school."

"Attach a photo to an email. She'll remember. And she'll be flattered."

"You're kidding. Flattered for what?"

"For receiving a little attention."

"I'd feel embarrassed. I already do."

"Josh, I admit, it's an audacious plan. But since when have you shrunk from audacity? If anyone can make this work, you're the one."

"Spare me!"

"Look at it this way: You have tomorrow off. You might

as well have a little fun, right? Earn a little money. Help me out in my career. What's not to like? All you have to do is tap Maryanne McCloskey for a little information about Robyn Templeton."

A pause followed. Robert pictured his friend wrestling with the proposition. "Okay," he said at last. "Okay, I'll do it. What the heck?"

"That's the Josh I know! You should be paying me for this, buddy."

"Don't push it."

SUNDAY:
GONE FISHIN'

Poblano pulled his Camry into the same empty lot he had used the previous day, his tires crunching over the gravel as he executed a U-turn to face the avenue. Before them, across the avenue, "Trash Be Gone!" swung into the center of the windshield like the main target on a firing range. The engine turned off, Poblano withdrew the key from the ignition, and the peace of a cloudless May morning descended upon them amid the chatter of young birds and the quiet rush along the avenue of an occasional passing vehicle.

"Everybody's sleeping," Poblano said. "Either that or recovering from a hangover."

It was early for a Sunday. Robert glanced at his phone. *8:12. People were probably sleeping late. But not everyone.* He noticed a young woman in a hospital uniform crossing the avenue, walking briskly toward a parked car, possibly a nurse heading to work. In general, though, the sidewalks and streets were deserted. "What do we do now?" he asked.

"Just watch," Poblano replied, nodding at Sánchez's place fifty yards away, visible in the center of the windshield. "I want to see who comes and who goes."

Robert sighed. Unlike the day before, they'd both come in casual dress, Robert wearing a short-sleeved shirt, cotton pants, and a pair of old running shoes. Still, the next several hours promised to be an ordeal. "We might be watching a long time," he remarked.

"Maybe. And maybe we won't see anything. But whether we do or not, we'll learn something."

Unconvinced, the young man looked the other way, out the side window to his right. He saw the fence again and a mild shudder passed through him. What he had taken the previous day for a spoiled head of cauliflower turned out to be a dead opossum. The carcass was crawling with flies, the winged insects furiously at work on the sabbath.

Poblano reached down beneath the dashboard for a thermos. "Want some coffee? It's real, not instant. Straight Colombian, not that flavored crap you get at Starbucks."

"No, thanks."

"I've got paper cups in the trunk."

"No, really," Robert protested, "I'm not thirsty. You keep paper cups in your trunk?"

"They're from a trip Gloria and I took with the kids last summer. There's some paper plates and plastic utensils back there too. Boy, that was a hell of a trip! We went up to one of those little lakes in Wisconsin and, on the way, I blew a tire. Had to get out the old jack and do the tire change right there at the side of the road." Poblano chuckled. "Remember that old Beatle song, 'Why Don't We Do It in the Road'?"

Robert frowned. "No," he shook his head.

"Ah, you're too young! Anyway, we were going up to the Badger State because I like to fish. Gloria likes to picnic. And the kids love the outdoors… At least they used to. Tommy and Sam still do. But the others…" Poblano shrugged. "They spend all their time plugged into these things." He held up his smartphone accusingly.

Robert's attention tapered off quickly. Soon he was no

longer hearing the words but only the sound of his mentor's voice, a smooth, quiet, baritone voice that blended easily into the serenity of the morning.

"What was Josh doing?" he wondered. He checked his phone: a quarter to nine. *Was he still asleep? Possibly. Knowing Josh...*

In the light of day, what had seemed a stroke of genius the night before seemed embarrassingly juvenile now, a wacko scheme Tom Sawyer might have concocted, not the product of an adult mind. *What if Poblano found out about it?* Robert shuddered at the thought. *The detective wouldn't like it. In fact, he'd be appalled by it, offended that Robert had gone behind his back to execute it. He might quit the mentorship.*

And if that happened, how would Robert explain it to his father? *After dropping out of the sociology program! After dicking around for three more years, first as a phlebotomist then as management trainee for the same grocery-store chain that had recently hired Josh.* Sensing another dead-end pending, he experienced a surge of desperation, a panicky desire to text his friend and order him to call the whole thing off.

"Do you have to pee?"

Startled, the young man looked at his mentor. "Wha... what was that?"

In the same quiet, calm, baritone voice he had used the first time, Poblano repeated the question. "You look a bit antsy," he added.

"Na... no. I'm fine."

"Well, if you do have to pee, you can do it right over there by the fence, behind that big tree. I'm sure folks around here won't mind."

An hour passed. A few cars went by. The flies labored on at

whatever they were doing. The sun inched its way up into the sky. The beaches wouldn't officially open until Memorial Day, but probably lots of people were already on the sand, strolling along the lakefront. Robert pictured the crowds basking in the sunshine at Oak Street Beach. After a protracted winter of freezing rain, snow, slushy sidewalks and gray skies, Chicagoans couldn't wait to get back to their beaches.

Through the corner of his eye, he noticed Poblano, relaxed, sipping from his coffee mug. *Perhaps dreaming about fishing.*

Another hour passed. An hour more. The sun rose above the treetops. It was warming the gravel of the lot now and turning the Camry's beige roof into a stove top on which eggs could be fried. Robert checked his phone again. No message.

Noon passed. Still no message. *Surely, Maryanne McClosky didn't need all afternoon to spill the beans on anyone.* But what did he know? Maybe she'd had a religious conversion or an epiphany or something like that and renounced gossip. *People changed. Sometimes.*

But assuming she was like most people and still approximated the person she was a few years ago, Josh wouldn't want to spend a minute longer with her than necessary. Robert pressed the soles of his running shoes against the panel under the dashboard, straining to stretch his legs. "How do we know when we've spent enough time here?"

Poblano sighed. "You young people! You've lost the ability to concentrate. Nobody perseveres anymore. And it's because of these." He held up his smartphone again and shook it.

"We've been here *five hours*," Robert noted.

"And we'll be here another five if the job calls for it. Have you ever gone fishing?"

"No."

"You should try it. In fishing, patience is a virtue. I've got a hunch about this Sánchez guy, and I'm going to follow up on it."

"A hunch?" Robert thought. *How about a bias, a bias against Hispanics?*

He glanced at his phone and this time his heart skipped a beat. A message. From Josh.

"Do you mind if I step out a moment?" he tried to sound nonchalant. "I think I do need to pee."

"No problem."

Robert exited the car and sauntered over to the end of the fence to a shady spot beneath a poplar tree that looked older than Methuselah. With his legs spread and his back to the Camry, he pecked at his phone with bated breath. "You were right about LaCroix," the text began.

She's up for tenure. At the end of the autumn semester. Which gives her just a few months. By 14 December, the committee must decide between her and another candidate. The political science department wanted to keep both professors but the administration is trying to save money. The usual story. They've eliminated a position, so that means one of these candidates, maybe LaCroix, must get the axe.

But here's the surprise: Templeton is not the other candidate. She took a new job at the U. of Wisconsin, Madison. She'll be gone by August.

LaCroix's rival is Marla Davis. Ever hear of her?

Regarding your second question, it seems that the only person who might have been on the premises Friday evening, the evening that LaCroix came back to her office, was a custodian named Rudenko. Nicholas Rudenko. He's scheduled to be back on duty Monday morning at Wilkinson Hall if you want to talk with him.

Whew! Glad I'm done with this. One lunch with Maryanne McClosky is enough!

So, when do I get paid?

Your friend (I think),

Josh

MONDAY: CONNECTING THE DOTS

Lying might be a sin. In fact, it was a sin. But sometimes you had to lie for the greater good, didn't you? This was the line of thought running through Robert's mind early Monday morning as he adjusted his necktie, put on his dress shoes, and picked up his phone to tap out a message to his mentor.

He was very sorry, the message said, but he could not meet with Poblano that morning on account of a stomachache. The gastrointestinal upset had started shortly after they left the Mexican restaurant where they ate following their surveillance of "Trash Be Gone!" The stomachache only worsened after nightfall. Now, at 6 a.m., he felt a lot better but terribly drained. He'd need the day to recuperate. Sorry. Very sorry.

With a spring in his step, the young man left his apartment, took a train to Hyde Park, and emerged from the electrically lit, dungeon-like station into the bright air of a glorious May morning. The breeze off the lake and even the exhaust fumes that tainted it smelled good to him, and like an elixir, they had a tonic effect, quickening the pace with which he hastened on to the campus. Poblano would thank him for this later, he thought. His unauthorized excursion, once it came to light, might even stir the envy of the seasoned investigator. *Imagine that!*

But surely, he thought, fate had something in store for him to punish him for his rebelliousness. It always seemed to work that way. Surely something would go wrong. Yet even as he entered Wilkinson Hall, luck stayed with him. As if in a dream, the maintenance man came around a corner, steering his yellow bucket across the tiles.

"Nicholas Rudenko?" Robert called out.

The man stopped and turned. He looked scared.

Robert smiled, anxious to establish the rapport on which further questioning would depend, but the man remained tense, as if braced for an attack. "I'd just like to ask a few questions. I'm a private investigator—"

"Look," the man cut in, "if this is about them alimony payments, I made the one for last month and I'll make the one for this month. If the bitch is asking for more, she can talk with my lawyer. I'm through with this bullshit!" He raised his voice, inadvertently drawing the attention of a couple of students on their way to classes.

Robert felt embarrassed both for Rudenko and for himself. The fiery outburst knocked him off course, leaving him with the ridiculous sense that he had somehow caused it.

He forced a smile and waved a hand apologetically, his heart pounding as he noticed the alarmed students turn away and hasten on down the hall. "I have nothing to do with... with any of that. I just want to ask a question about a professor here at the university, Ilona LaCroix. Do you know her?"

Rudenko softened a bit.

Robert forced another smile. "I have reason to believe that you may have seen her Friday evening."

"Friday evening?"

"You were at work here at that time, I believe."

Rudenko searched his memory. "Yeah, that's right," he nodded. "I work a couple other jobs too, but I was here that night. Here and in that hall across the courtyard, Barley Hall."

"Around seven or eight?"

"That's the time it would have been, yeah."

"Did you see anyone who stands out in memory?"

He looked at Robert, not puzzled but calculating, as if debating how to reply. "Yes, I did," he said, keeping his eyes on Robert, gauging his reaction. "In Barley Hall. That professor you mentioned. I think I might have seen her."

"She's fairly young, between 25 and 35 years of age?"

"That sounds about right."

Robert looked more closely at Rudenko, the man's face a composite of Slavic features, a broad nose, and a certain bulldoggish aspect. He appeared about 45 years of age. "Did she talk with you?"

"Not much. She was in a rush."

"A 'rush'?"

"She was running. Quite a sight! A woman in high heels running toward me. I heard her before I saw her. Of course, I looked up from my work."

"She stopped to talk with you?"

"She sure did. She stopped pretty fast too. Almost slipped. And she was..." He mimicked rapid respiration.

"Panting?"

"Yeah, that's right. Panting. She wanted to know if I had seen anything."

"What do you mean?"

"That was *my* question. I didn't know what she was talking about. She asked if I'd seen anyone carrying a computer. Maybe carrying other things too, like speakers, a printer, books... She said someone had taken all her stuff out of her office." He laughed, rubbing his stubbly chin. "She was in a panic."

"What did you tell her?"

Rudenko seemed to shrink from the question, his guardedness rising up again like the pikes of a phalanx. "Look, mister, I don't know what this is about."

He eyed Robert's necktie then glanced down at his newly polished Oxford shoes. "I didn't know about any robbers, either. I have nothing to do with shit like that. No way!" he shook his head. "If somebody took her stuff, then that's on them. All I did was what I was asked to do and what I was paid to do."

Robert was intrigued. "What were you paid to do?"

"Just open a door, that's all. Just open a door."

"What door?"

"To a certain office, so some Mexicans could haul some junk away. That's all I did. And that's all *they* did, as far as I know. If they stole anything, it's on them. I don't know anything about it. I had nothing to do with it."

While Rudenko was professing his innocence, Robert could feel his own heart pounding, like that of an archeologist on the threshold of unearthing a precious but extraordinarily fragile find, terrified that even just one wrong, hasty move might ruin it forever. "*Who* paid you?"

Rudenko stopped talking, stopped rattling on about his innocence, and bowed his head like a schoolboy ashamed of something. "I can't say."

"You can't say?"

"I don't know her name."

Robert whipped out his phone and displayed two photos taken from the university's website. "Do you recognize her?"

The custodian looked at the photos. "She's the one," his smudged fingertip touched the face he claimed to recognize.

"You sure it wasn't this one?" Robert indicated the photo of Templeton.

"Of course, I'm sure. *She's* the one." He pointed again at the other photo, the one of Marla Davis. "She said it was an extra duty she was asking of me and I deserved extra compensation. She even gave me the key, so I could open the door."

She had probably also enjoined him to keep quiet about it, Robert thought. He must be betraying her now. *While exploiting his deviousness, she'd underestimated it!*

On the other hand, what did it matter? If he ratted on her, she'd simply deny involvement or make up lies to cover her tracks. If it came to a question of her word versus his—a respected professor's word against that of a maintenance man—there was no doubt whom the administration would believe. There was no doubt which one of them would enjoy its support and which one would get the shaft.

"What did she pay you?" Robert asked, genuinely curious.

"That's a bit nosy, mister, don't you think? Who did you say you were?"

"A private investigator." Robert felt a bit queasy, aware of how far he was from earning his license.

"Let's just say it made the 'extra duty' worthwhile," Rudenko said. He looked down, averting his eyes, as if he had something more to say. *Like a lizard who'd swallowed something indigestible but was having trouble vomiting it out.*

"Are you telling me everything?" Robert asked.

The custodian made no reply, avoiding eye contact.

"She's missing, you know. I'm trying to find her. That's what this is about."

Rudenko looked up, mildly alarmed. "What do you mean she's missing?"

"She's disappeared. Kidnapped maybe. Maybe worse."

The custodian blew air out through his mouth, exhaling as if to relieve a build-up of internal pressure, and his knuckles whitened around the mop handle. "Okay, I'll tell you. You know Orlov's Electronics Shop?"

"Never heard of it."

Rudenko gave an address. "It's a crumby neighborhood, mostly Hispanic, some Black, a few old Polacks hanging on. I told her the guys who cleared out her office took her computer there."

"To Orlov's?"

"Yeah, that's right."

Robert was puzzled. "How did you know they were going there?"

"I didn't."

"You didn't?"

"No."

"Then why did you tell her that?"

He shrugged. "No reason, I guess."

Robert felt the blood drain from his face. *The reason is you're an asshole, a perverse, misogynistic asshole.*

Rudenko slid a dirty, gray sleeve across his face and grinned, revealing a mouthful of heavily stained teeth. "You should have seen her, though. She took off down the hall like a racehorse in those high heels of hers." He began quaking with laughter. "The prof chasing the Mexicans!" Apparently unable to suppress his sense of humor, he went on laughing, his face reddening. Then suddenly he stopped, noticing that Robert was not joining in the merriment, and adopted a serious look. "I… I hope nothing's happened to her, though. Nothing bad I mean."

The young man shook his head in disgust and, turning away, left the maintenance man to his mop and bucket.

* * *

Google Maps showed Orlov's Electronics Shop about half a mile down the commercial avenue from "Trash Be Gone!" In the Honda Civic his Uncle Declan had given him a year ago as a birthday present, Robert had no trouble finding the place. He parked the car just outside the shop and surveyed the neighborhood.

In the sunshine, it looked safe enough, free of those aspects which, after dark, would have warned passersby to steer clear of the mouths of alleys, give wide berths to the street corners, and avoid strangers. Even so, Robert noticed a curious incident. A young Black man, a lanky fellow, was leaning against a brick wall near a vacated storefront, apparently sipping from a bottle wrapped in a tall, slender, brown paper bag. Further down the block, a pair of Hispanic girls appeared, spotted the Black man and abruptly changed course, crossing over to the other side of the street. *Better safe than sorry.*

Robert looked at the shop itself. Beneath the "Orlov's Electronics" sign appeared the not-quite-washed-away letters of a predecessor, "Artisanal Fruits and Vegetables." Either Orlov was too lazy to finish redoing the front or he had calculated that the place would not endure long enough to make the job worthwhile. To the left of the shop lay a vacancy, the windows soaped over with a sign reading "Office Space Available." To the right was a defunct pizza place, its sign still announcing, "Open 11 a.m. to midnight. FREE DELIVERY!"

Orlov's itself was dark and smelled of sawdust, the floor

made of narrow wooden boards like the kind in grocery stores from the 1950's. Every step elicited a creaking sound, suggesting that some unfortunate customer might one day break through the floor and land in the basement. Despite the dazzling sunlight just outside the window, perpetual dusk seemed to permeate the interior, obscuring everything behind the counter, including the man who stood there, watching as Robert approached.

"You have order to pick up?" Speaking with a pronounced Slavic accent, he looked like bouncer, stocky, with a round, beefy face, broad nose and thick lips, his pate as bare as a billiard ball.

"Are you from Russia?" Robert asked, hoping to strike an amicable chord.

"Belarus," came the gruff reply. "You want maybe to drop something off? We take everything." He spread his arms. "Computers. Printers. Speakers. Webcams. Monitors. Batteries. Everything electronic we take!"

"In return for what?" Robert kept up the exchange, unsure how he would put his main question, the question burning inside him—the only question that had brought him there.

"We pay fair price," Orlov replied. "Usually, old stuff not worth much. But for everything we pay."

"And what do you *do* with the stuff after you pay for it?"

The man's eyes narrowed. "Are you from city?"

"No."

"State?"

"No." Robert smiled. "I'm not from the government. I'm just doing a little research. For myself."

"A student?" Orlov eyed him skeptically.

"From the university," Robert nodded. *Why not? Let him*

think I'm a student. "I'm just curious to know how electronics items are disposed of. I happened to be in the neighborhood. I saw your place and so…"

Orlov shrugged. "Nothing much to it. Mostly, we take stuff apart, sometimes put back together, sometimes resell." He stopped talking, as if suddenly aware of a possible threat. "Look, if you have nothing to sell and want nothing to buy, then I have work to do."

"Do you recall a young woman who came by here Friday evening?" Robert blurted out, his heart pounding. "A professional-looking woman. In a business suit. High heels. With a handbag."

"I had more than one customer."

"But this was a young woman, late twenties, early thirties, between about a quarter to eight and nine o'clock Friday night. In a business skirt. High heels. By herself."

Surely, he didn't get many customers like that, Robert thought. *Not at that hour. Not at a place like this…*

Orlov pretended to be puzzled. "What are you saying? My place not safe? Not attractive?"

Robert laughed. "What do *you* think? This isn't exactly Mister Rogers' Neighborhood."

Orlov looked nonplussed. "Mister Rogers?"

"Forget it," Robert snapped, leaning over the counter. "Just tell me. Do you remember this woman? Two nights ago. Friday night."

Orlov stared at him.

"Please tell me. I am looking for her."

Orlov nodded. "Yes, I do remember woman like one you describe. She gets out of taxi in front of store. Comes in. Excited. Asks about computer. Wants to pick up computer.

But I have nothing for her. No order. No computer. Nothing. Very strange. And very excited, this woman." He paused, recollecting the odd encounter, his recollections comporting with those of Rudenko. How excited this woman had been!

"So, what happened?"

Orlov shrugged. "She leaves."

"That's it?"

"That's it."

"Where did she go?"

Orlov emitted a glum laugh. "Look out window." He pointed to the street. "What do you see? Lots of cars. People walking. It was dark. She left store. After that, who knows?"

A quizzical look appeared on his beefy face. "Ah!" he said, producing a sleazy smile. "Is she… is she maybe your girlfriend?"

Robert turned away, aimed like a thunderbolt at the exit. Inside his car he checked his messages. Poblano had texted him. "Best wishes for a speedy recovery, kid."

Recovery? Ah, yes, I'm recovering from an upset stomach—the most delightful one I've ever had!

In fact, he could hardly contain his jubilation. It all made sense now.

Wishing to eliminate her rival, Davis promised to pay the maintenance man if he misdirected the junk haulers to clear out LaCroix's office instead of Hamilton's, thereby sabotaging LaCroix's research. To earn his pay, Rudenko needed to redirect Sánchez who, acting on Templeton's instructions, had already begun clearing out Hamilton's office.

After Templeton left, Rudenko seized his opportunity, moved in and persuaded Sánchez a mistake had been made. The men laughed over it, perhaps deriding the "snooty"

Templeton, professors in general, or women in general for thinking they knew everything. After their jocular exchange, Rudenko departed and Sánchez and crew turned their efforts away from Hamilton's office toward LaCroix's.

Hours later, LaCroix showed up. Panicking, she turned south, not north the way she had come, because she wanted to find someone, anyone, who might be inside one of the offices and provide information about her lost belongings. Alas, all the doors were locked!

Quitting the third floor, she ran downstairs and out the south exit of Wilkinson Hall, across the quadrangle and into neighboring Barley Hall, still desperate to find someone, anyone, who might help her when she bumped into the maintenance man. Rudenko, out of depraved indifference, misdirected her, causing her to make a fruitless trip to Orlov's shop.

Back at the Berghoff, Davis, having intended only to impede LaCroix's research, was alarmed over her colleague's failure to rejoin her at the restaurant. Suspecting something dreadful—something to which she herself might have inadvertently contributed—she hired Poblano to look into the matter.

Robert's thoughts swung back to Rudenko, in particular to his showing up at the north end of the third floor of Wilkinson Hall on Saturday morning. According to Templeton, he should not have been there at all. Why then was he there? Why, wasn't it obvious? To savor the fruits of his foul play by viewing LaCroix's empty office!

And Orlov? Orlov might be the moral equivalent of a shady used-car salesman, but he had probably spoken honestly regarding LaCroix, telling all he knew about his brief encounter with her. His story added a piece to Rudenko's while shedding little light on where she was now.

Only one question remained: When should Robert disclose all this to Poblano? Immediately? Or should he wait until they met again? Given the bombshell nature of what he had discovered, he decided to wait, having no idea that everything he had just learned, accurate as it all was, was about to be eclipsed.

* * *

Seated inside a rounded garret little larger than a walk-in closet, Ilona LaCroix stared stoically at the wall in front of her, trying to maintain a dignified façade as fingers not her own pressed a wad of cloth into her mouth. The sticky, polythene underside of standard gray duct tape met the delicate skin of her face and still she made no protest. Like an Olympian goddess carved out of marble, she continued to sit amid the ugly snarls of the tape as it was peeled off its roll and wrapped around her jaws, the back of her neck, and below the bun of her hair.

"Just stay quiet," they told her.

Eager to comply, she continued staring at the wall as a white neckerchief, pilfered from her handbag, was wrapped over the tape and knotted behind her neck.

"Just stay quiet," they told her, "and no one'll get hurt."

That was all they needed to tell her. If anyone's wellbeing depended on her staying quiet, Ilona LaCroix would stay quiet.

The gag, though, made it easier. It reduced their need to trust her and, in turn, relieved her of the pressure to keep showing how trustworthy she was. With the gag on, she could relax a little.

She, of course, would still need to trust *them*. She'd need to trust that they would follow through on their side of the bargain, if one could call it a bargain, namely that they'd notify the person whose name and address she had divulged so that they could arrange to have her rescued without requiring anyone to call the police.

Howsoever much they despised the larger community, they still retained a healthy respect for the police. Perhaps it was more fear than respect.

They would never admit to fear. Indeed, they expressed as much contempt for the cops as they did for everyone else, but she heard the truth in their voices. She could see it now as they prepared to depart—the nervous glances they cast at their phones, the tense manner in which they peeked out through the room's only window. *Like terrified watchmen on an exposed tower.*

The chair was set on the floorboards in the center of the room. They took care in tying her to it, remarkable care, balancing a desire to make a clean getaway against a desire to keep her alive and well.

The state could impose a life sentence for murder. Penalties for kidnapping were substantially less so long as the victim remained uninjured. Why risk spending the rest of their lives in prison if they could avoid it with a couple bundles of cheap, white, cotton clothesline and a roll of duct tape?

Almost from the moment she exited Orlov's electronics shop and was whisked away at gunpoint, she'd been wondering who her abductors were. Clearly having nothing to do with Orlov, they spoke Spanish, apparently unaware that she could understand every word. They kept referring to her as the gringo whore, the slutty moll of a guy named Delgado. *A rival gang member perhaps? Someone who had double-crossed them? Stolen from them? Insulted them?*

Whoever he was, he must have shown a weakness for a woman for whom she could be mistaken. A white woman. English-speaking. The kind of woman thugs might call "classy."

They suspected their mistake almost as soon as they made it. "I thought you said she had long, dark hair," one remarked.

Her hair was not all that long and it certainly wasn't dark. Still blindfolded, her hands zip-tied behind her back, she shook her head when they asked her if she colored it.

They tried questioning her in English, crudely, ineptly, clumsily. Feigning incomprehension, she protested in English that she couldn't understand them—a protestation that must have struck them as entirely plausible, given the quality of their English.

Frustrated, they removed the blindfold. Dazzled by the light, she squinted back at them as they studied her face from behind their black ski masks. "I think it's her," the one holding the lamp concluded.

"It *better* be her."

"How could it *not* be?"

They looked at a phone, at her, then back at the phone, comparing her to Delgado's girlfriend. "I don't know," one shook his head.

"Who else could she be, then? Castillo gave us all the information. Right place. Right time. Right dress."

"It was getting dark."

"But we could see! We can see *now!*"

Hoping against hope, they ran their eyes over her, straining to match her appearance with that of the woman in the photo. Sitting on the floor against the wall, she shrank beneath their scrutiny, embarrassed, her hands still zip-tied behind her.

She could feel their eyes on every part of her as they examined her attire. The lily-white blouse. The navy-blue business skirt. The russet-brown nylons. The shiny, black pumps. Breasts. Legs. Feet. Every part of her!

"Let's just assume it's her."

"Damn it, it *is* her!"

They spent Saturday and Sunday trying to prove a lie, to confirm an impossibility, to convince themselves of something that could never be. Meanwhile, they treated her fairly well, all things considered. Minutes after the blindfold came off, they freed her hands, and she was never tied up again—until now.

Now, though, they did a thorough job. Fastening her to the chair, they trussed her up from shoulders to ankles before fixing that lollapalooza of a gag over her mouth. They kept adding. Augmenting. Supplementing. *Like researchers forever doubting the validity of their findings!* Only when convinced that she'd remain quiet, both safe and secured, were they satisfied with their handiwork. Only then did they flee.

She pictured them hastening downstairs, one following the other, down two flights of stairs to the street behind the house. Their departure felt like the breaking of a fever. Relief dawned, relief as broad as the firmament, as deep as the ocean: She was alone! For the first time in days. Alone. Unwatched. Unmonitored. *No more need to show compliance. No more need to avert her eyes. No more need to...*

A teardrop formed and oozed out to be absorbed by the cloth wrapped over her mouth. *Hallelujah! Praise the Lord!*

She heard the sound of traffic in the street. From where?

A block away? Three blocks? Although she'd been aware of it before, it sounded different now. Not like white noise anymore but soothing beyond belief, like the rush of a brook tumbling over rocks in the green shade of an ancient forest. She felt she could listen to that sound forever. *A balm to her soul.*

But she was wrong.

Broken only by the occasional honk of a horn or the siren of a passing ambulance, the rush of the traffic soon grew monotonous. And a new fear rose within her: the fear that she might drowse off before her rescuers arrived.

Determined to stay awake, she took to playing mental games, challenging herself to recall pieces of music, pop tunes, poetry, and phrases from famous speeches. She tried meditating, visualizing pleasant things like flowers and butterflies, fields of wheat, sunrises over Lake Michigan.

She thought a lot too. She thought about her grandfather and her life with him. She thought about how proud her parents would be, had they lived to see her graduate *summa cum laude*. She thought about her friends, her colleagues, and—although she tried not to think of him—Daniel.

They must all be sick with worry. How much pain she was causing!

Not that she'd ever intended to hurt anyone, but who was it who thrust her into the circumstances that led to all this? *To go running after a computer? Into a strange neighborhood? After dusk? Unaccompanied? And for what? To finish a research paper on the propensities of Catalonian voters to…*

Oh, what did it matter!

Feeling bitter, she stopped thinking and a sense of curiosity welled up in her. She began testing her bonds. Not that she had any illusions of being able to free herself but twisting and turning gave her something else to do, a new diversion from discomfiting thoughts, another way to keep boredom at bay.

Twisting and turning, though, brought on another affliction: perspiration. Dampening her clothing, it made her irritable and ornery and reminded her that she hadn't had a bath or change of clothes in three days. Had her kidnappers not allowed her to remove her shoes before binding her to the chair, she'd be burning up now, ready to combust.

And that chair! She couldn't curse it enough. A plain, armless, artless little thing made of cheap wood with a round wicker seat, it was the sort of chair one might see at a table in an outdoor café, easily lifted by any waitress and carried with one hand. Yet with her in it, bound as she was, she could hardly budge. Nor could she steer the chair in any sensible direction without risking toppling over—a prospect she dreaded.

Her nyloned feet, tied ankle-to-ankle, were drawn back beneath the seat. With rope holding her legs together at the knees, crisscrossing her lap, gripping her waist, and embracing her chest, she could hardly move. Stretching was impossible; bending, out of the question. Thus, woven to the chair and anchored to the spot, she decided to focus on her hands. Just her hands. It made eminent sense theoretically. If she could but free her hands, she could undo the knot over her stomach, unwrap the ropes around her lap, unwind the ones around her legs, remove the ones around her ankles, and...

Ah, but that was just the thing! She couldn't free her hands. Bound heel-to-heel, they remained joined behind the back of the chair, permanently so it seemed, until someone should come along to undo *that* knot—the one standing guard, as it were, over her would-be liberating fingers.

After this reality sank in, she gave up, relaxing entirely.

What was the use? Time dragged. *Let it drag!* And it did drag. More slowly, it seemed, than she'd ever experienced it. Or perhaps not quite. She recalled the lectures of a certain professor she'd had in undergraduate school. *Better to be tied to a chair than endure one of HIS lectures!*

Not really, though. Not in her current circumstances.

With the window shut and shaded, the air in the room was stagnant, and the woody smell of the floorboards grew unnaturally intense. She felt the heat of the afternoon rise. Fearing she might faint, she slumped forward, face down, resting on the balls of her feet.

Then something startled her, straightening her up, and she returned to full wakefulness—boys! They seemed to have sprung out of nowhere, yelling, heckling, ribbing each other. They were bouncing a basketball. She listened, heart pounding in the dimmed light of the room, picturing them in an alley behind the building, catching, passing, jumping, and scrambling, just two floors beneath her bound feet.

Strangely inspired, she began tugging again at the rope holding her ankles back. Was there really no way to break free? Picturing the boys passing, jumping, dodging and leaping, she strained, tugged, twisted and turned, causing the chair to squeak and creak beneath her. Like a butterfly straining to burst its cocoon, could she not burst her bonds by dint of sheer force?

Then suddenly she quit. What was the use? She had gained nothing except to make the chair squeak, and its squeaking made her feel it was laughing at her.

Outside, the boys played on, oblivious of her distress. Oblivious of *her*. She closed her eyes.

When she awoke, the light in the room had changed.

Could she have slept through the night? Was this a new day? An odd mixture of hope and alarm welled up in her.

But no. It was still Monday. The same insufferably endless Monday afternoon in which she seemed inescapably trapped.

She recovered her bearings. The sun was setting. That's why the light in the room had changed. The sun's rays were beating directly against the room's only window. Soon it would dip below the horizon. Dusk would thicken. Night would fall. Then only the pale glow of the streetlights would seep around the edges of the window shade, alleviating, albeit not much, the darkness inside.

She listened for the boys, but they were gone. Probably long gone. The alley was quiet. The rush of the traffic was all she heard. And the room was cooler. Her nylons were dry again. *Something to be grateful for!*

In the breezes along the lakefront and inland, lilacs were scenting the air. Amid the salty, sultry smells inside her cramped prison, she imagined the fragrances of the white and purple blooms and, thinking of them, thought of her friend, the one whose name she had divulged. The one on whom she was counting.

Marla would know what to do! Marla would know whom to call!

* * *

Shortly after nightfall, the Toyota Camry arrived, inadvertently pulling into a parking space where someone had smashed a liquor bottle on the sidewalk. Exiting from the passenger's side, Robert crunched onto the glassy shards, feeling them grind like scrimshaw between the concrete and his shoe. He felt something else too: dampness in his armpits. The night was warm and humid, but the cause of his perspiration had nothing to do with the weather.

"You all right?" Poblano asked.

"Yeah, I'm fine."

"I wasn't sure you could make it on such short notice."

"I've had all day to recuperate."

"Sorry about that burrito."

The young man smiled. "I'm not sure it was that."

"Yeah, it was. I should report those dirty spics to the health department. I bet half of 'em are illegals."

"I thought you liked the tacos."

"I like the tamales too, but I'm never going there again."

Robert said nothing about his escapades earlier that day, of what he had learned thanks partly to Josh but mainly to his own bold initiative. This was no time to reveal his maverick streak and sharing his newfound intelligence could wait. The priority now was to find Ilona.

Poblano had parked just north of a commercial avenue that ran east-west. Crossing the avenue walking south, Robert glanced left, impressed by the colored lights that, in the distance, appeared not spaced out at intervals as they really were, but jammed up together, resembling clustered ornaments in a luminescent collage. Red, green, and yellow traffic signals blinked on and off over the roadway while neon signs adorned the sidewalks, some flashing amid the changing traffic signals. Augmenting this multicolored light show were the headlights and taillights of moving cars and the coppery hue of the streetlights, the entire avenue shining like a bejeweled serpent fluorescing beneath the clouds, its artificial radiance staining their billowy undersides.

Various enterprises lined the avenue: a liquor store, a food mart, a Persian rug shop, doughnut shop, pizza place, ice cream parlor, a Chinese restaurant and... Something in the distance caught his eye. Robert squinted to sharpen his vision. In red neon letters, tiny but clear, appeared the name: ORLOV'S.

"What is it?" Poblano looked in the same direction.

"Na... nothing. I'm just surprised that... that so much business goes on after dark."

Poblano laughed. "We ain't in Iowa, kid."

They reached the parkway on the other side and Poblano turned around. Mimicking his mentor, Robert looked back also. "You think we're being followed?"

"Naw, not really. I'm just worried about the car. Maybe that wasn't the best place to park. But then, where *is* a good place in *this* neighborhood?" Poblano rolled his eyes.

Robert recalled the recent spree of thefts in which the thieves, specializing in catalytic converters, fell upon parked vehicles and made off with the highly coveted car parts.

Heading south, they passed a house that looked gutted. Its timbers were charred, its upper-floor windows missing, and part of a sloping roof had caved in, crumbling onto the floor below. Robert didn't recall hearing of a local fire on the news. *But then probably a lot happened that never made it into the news.*

In front of them on the right lay a series of bungalows that, in the sepia-toned radiance of the streetlights, resembled images in a daguerreotype. Lights were on above doorways and inside living rooms. People were at home.

Beyond the bungalows yawned an open space the size of a football field. Enclosed by a crosswire fence, this empty lot separated the bungalows from a very different structure, a three-story house made of red sandstone. It had an aristocratic look. Rising above the corner of the block, it stood bathed in the light of the streetlights on the side overlooking the street but veiled in shadows on the other side, the side facing the lot. The first and second floor windows, tall and rectangular, were pitch black, suggesting the house had been vacated.

There was another window, though, one on the third floor, which differed in character. Smaller and square-shaped, it was embedded in the convex outer wall of a tower-like structure with a conical roof. A shade had been drawn over it. Like the pale surface of a movie screen, the shade reflected the coppery glow of a nearby streetlight. According to an anonymous note that had appeared mysteriously on Davis's doorstep, LaCroix should be inside the room behind that window.

"She's probably tied up," Poblano said, "but she should be okay. I hope so." He didn't sound too confident.

Excited at the prospect of finding her missing friend, Davis had wanted to accompany them, but Poblano, much to Robert's relief, forbad it. The detective expected no trouble, he told her, but if trouble arose, he wanted her out of it. She could stay about a mile away, which is where she was now, at a table inside a burger joint, anxiously awaiting their report.

"As I recall," Poblano said, "the alderperson in this ward wanted this place torn down, but the City Council has been too busy promoting the Obama Library, cassinos, pot sales, and our sanctuary-city status. Things get neglected, kid."

He looked again at the red sandstone house with its castle-like features. "Nice workplace, though, for thugs who value style."

Robert bit his lip. "You still think we shouldn't call the police?"

Poblano sighed. "Honestly, I don't know. I'm trying to play it safe here. If she's really up there—and I don't even know if she is—and if whoever tipped off Davis finds out that we called the cops, what do you think the bad guys might do?"

Robert looked at his mentor, the men locking eyes, no longer as teacher to student but as man to man.

"Some pretty ugly things," Poblano answered his own question. "Characters like that have ways of finding out how things go and also ways of coming back to haunt you. It appears they've done us a little favor, sending that note. I wouldn't want to overtax their goodwill."

"I... I understand," Robert murmured, aware once more of the dampness in his armpits.

"This is a very unusual case, kid—not the kind I would have preferred to introduce you to the profession. You don't need to go further. You can go back to the car if you like."

Robert shook his head vehemently.

"Okay then, let's go."

They approached the building. "I've been in this area before," Poblano noted. "A couple of years ago. Had to collect a debt. There's an alley in the back. If we have to smash a window to get in, that's the place to do it. You have your sidearm?"

"Yes, of course." His lips dry, Robert reached under the flap of his jacket for the waistband and touched the weapon in the holster.

"Stay alert now."

Behind them, a sports utility vehicle slowed down, coming almost to a stop, then crawled toward them along the curb. Robert noticed it in the corner of his eye and, curious, turned to see. Poblano, puzzled at first, also looked. Then his eyes opened wide. He whipped out his handgun and yelled for Robert to duck behind a parked car.

It all happened so fast. Shots rang out. Tires screeched. The vehicle sped away into the night. Poblano got the license-plate number then came out from behind the parked car. Robert had crumpled onto the grass along the curb.

As the county coroner would later determine, the young man died instantly, robbed of a future by a single 9-millimeter bullet tearing a lethal path through the tender tissues of the neocortex.

GHOST AT THE BANQUET

Following the funeral Mass at old St. Pat's, the mourners drove up Ashland Avenue to Graceland Cemetery for the burial ceremony then on to the White Eagle reception hall in Niles for the memorial luncheon. The large number of attendees surprised Detective Poblano, but it was not the only thing that surprised him: Half of those in attendance looked Mexican. In fact, they were not Mexican, although they were Hispanic, but since Poblano couldn't tell Venezuelans from Puerto Ricans, Colombians from Salvadorans, they all looked Mexican to him.

As the detective learned only at the funeral, Robert's mother was born in Ecuador. His father, of Irish descent, had arranged for some of the Latino side of the family to fly up from the home country to be with his wife at this difficult time.

"He must be loaded," Poblano thought to himself. *Wonder what he does for a living.* Camouflaged, as it were, in a group of diners at a table gleaming and glittering with porcelain plates, wine glasses, bottles, and silverware, the detective wiled away the time conducting furtive, long-distance studies of other guests.

Never a fan of large crowds and never comfortable in them, he avoided conversation, confining his talk mainly to the matronly woman with the pearl necklace sitting to his right, his wife Gloria. "Who'd have guessed his mother was from Ecuador," he whispered to her. "I thought he was one-hundred-percent Irish. I suppose, though, that some lighter-skinned Hispanics…"

Gloria had turned in the other direction, straining to catch an amusing anecdote told by a man with the shoulders of a football fullback, red hair, a rosy complexion, and a form of elocution marked by exclamatory inflections and an exaggerated Irish accent. With his formidable torso, booming voice, and boisterous laugh, he was holding the ladies at his end of the table riveted the way a circus clown might bedazzle a gathering of kindergartners.

Poblano hated him at first sight. *Guys like that—who did they think they were? God's gift to the world?*

There did, in fact, seem something indecent about it all: all that joking, all that laughter, all that food and drink. A young man had been killed, for heaven's sake!

A minute more of the blarney, and the detective could bear no more. Overriding an instinctive preference for invisibility, he rose from his chair, conspicuously abandoning a plate of filet mignon and a glass of excellent red wine. Where should he go? *Anywhere to get away from that over-inflated gas bag!*

He considered the restroom, the dance floor, the buffet table, even the parking lot and settled for the buffet table. Feigning interest in an array of nuts, dried fruits, cookies, cakes, pies, and puddings, he began to relax, and his thoughts turned inward. What a couple of weeks it had been! And now today… The service at the church. The gathering at the cemetery. His vision blurred and for a moment he neither saw nor heard anything around him. *So young! So enthusiastic. His first case! The very first! He took a handkerchief from his breast pocket.*

"Detective Poblano?" A timorous female voice interrupted his thoughts, a voice he recognized.

"Why, Professor LaCroix!"

"Sorry!" she blushed, "I didn't mean to…"

"To interrupt? I'm glad you did." He daubed his eyes briskly and returned the handkerchief to his breast pocket.

She was dressed in black, as were all the women. In church and at the cemetery, some had worn black veils that hung from headpieces, obscuring their faces. Nearly all had worn black pumps. Despite the warm spring weather, most had worn nylons too, mostly black. Only their gloves were white. White as snow. Little white gloves folded in prayer, resting on pews, clutching the straps of handbags…

"What a pleasant surprise!" he said. "I didn't even know you were here."

"How could I not be?" she smiled sweetly, sadly. "When I heard that a man had died trying to rescue me, I was…" She bowed her head and shuddered, her grief impossible to hide.

He put a hand on her shoulder. "We'll catch the animals who did it."

As he knew well, though, Robert's killers might never be caught, even though the stolen vehicle they had used had been recovered. They were probably just a bunch of kids out for a joy ride, having no more connection to their victim than LaCroix's kidnappers had to her. Since no one in the shooter's circle was likely to trust the police, it was doubtful that anyone would ever come forward to disclose anything. With new crimes occurring every day, the police would need to move on, and the case would go cold. *As cold as the corpse now lying at Graceland.*

"It's a shame," LaCroix murmured, daubing her eyes with a napkin.

The beauty of her face impressed him as never before. There was a somber, ethereal radiance to it now that never showed and perhaps never could show in a photograph, an ineffable sorrow that emanated from deep within her, surrounding her as if with a warm, golden aura. He was reminded of certain stone sculptures he had seen in graveyards on a trip through Europe years before, sculptures of angels, sculptures of the bereaved, sculpted figures who would never leave the cemetery.

Maybe that was it, he thought. The car accident that killed her parents and all her siblings—two brothers, two sisters. *Maybe that's what lay behind those sad, dark, olive eyes.* When he thought of her name, the Ionian islands came to mind. Deep blue waters. Warm breezes. Whisperings of ancient catastrophes long ago forgotten. *Ilona!*

"I can't help but feel," she said, "that... that somehow... to some degree... I am to blame."

Poblano stared at her, bewildered. "To blame? For what?" He was still thinking of the car accident.

"For Robert's death. I shouldn't have been where I was. I shouldn't have gone there that night."

Marveling at her admission, he tried to catch her eyes, but she kept her head bowed, her eyes averted. "Don't think that way. Please don't."

Yet he knew what she meant. He'd had the same feelings. *If only he hadn't called the young man that evening... If only he had ordered him to wait in the car... If only...*

But this was a stupid way of thinking. One could trace any disaster back to prior choices, even all the way back to the Garden of Eden and blame it on Adam and Eve. Or on whatever primordial humans were roaming about, basking in blissful, bestial innocence. But what good did such thinking do? What practical answers did it yield? What workable remedies did it ever suggest? He was aching to share something of this with her, but she kept her eyes down, lost in her own thoughts.

"It all seems so senseless," she whispered, shaking her head.

"It is," Poblano replied. "Maybe drugs had something to do with it. The shooter might have been high on something. Crack-cocaine's been a problem for decades, but there's this new thing called fentanyl. You may have heard of it."

"I have."

Poblano rambled on about the drug problem, glad to dwell on a topic that kept him away from Robert's death and the glum drift of his own unchanneled thoughts. "It's a synthetic opioid. A spoonful of the stuff could wipe out the whole population of Chicago, and it's coming up from Mexico. Dealers lace heroin with it. Half the time, the kids don't even know they're taking it."

"That's terrible."

"It is. And it's gonna wreck this country if we don't stop it. But, as we all know…" he sneered, "we don't have a crisis at the border."

Like the sun emerging through a break in the clouds, Daniel Bachmann appeared. He was wearing a three-piece suit in somber yet pleasant shades of brown, his pants creased, hair trimmed, and the knot of a gold necktie, perfectly shaped, resting just below his Adam's apple. He put an arm around LaCroix who immediately snuggled against him.

"We've made up," he said, addressing Poblano with a smile.

"I've gathered that."

"After what I'd been through," LaCroix said, "I… I thought…" She choked up. Bachmann gave her a squeeze. "I thought about a lot of things. My career. My… my life…" Her voice jumped up an octave.

Bachmann gave her another squeeze and she buried her face in his chest.

"We thank you, detective," he said. "We'll be forever grateful."

Poblano reached up, as if to lift the brim of a hat he was wearing, although he had nothing on his head except a partial covering of thinning brown hair streaked with gray. "I wish you well. Both of you."

A new voice invaded their company like a trumpet from four tables away. "Ilona!"

Marla Davis was approaching fast, picking her way in high heels through the crowded hall like a skilled navigator among the tables. A tall woman with long, chestnut-brown hair and prominent cheekbones, she had a nose that looked made for pecking into hard surfaces. Wrapped in a black satin gown that put her breasts on display, she looked like someone carrying a pair of honeydew melons strapped to her chest.

"Why, Detective Poblano!" she planted herself in front of him. "How nice to see you again!" Leaving him no chance to reply, she turned to LaCroix. "Ilona!"

"Oh, Marla!"

The women hugged.

"How *are* you, dear?"

"I'm fine."

"Are you sure?"

LaCroix nodded, her eyes glistening.

"Oh, you dear sweetie!" Davis hugged her again. "You've been through so much! I can hardly imagine what it must have been like. And I've been so worried about you. Days went by. I heard nothing. Then a week... I wanted to catch up with you at the church this morning, but..." She shook her head, as if remorseful about something. "I had to finish writing."

"Writing?"

"I've been writing a speech," Davis fluttered her elongated eyelashes.

"A speech?" Bachmann inquired. "About what?"

"It's an acceptance speech of sorts." Davis inhaled deeply, expanding her bust even beyond its natural proportions, held her breath to prolong the suspense then, like a thundercloud bursting, reported the news. "I got tenure!"

LaCroix brought her hand up to her mouth, as if the news had been too good to utter, even though it had just been announced loud and clear for all to hear. "Tenure! Oh, Marla!"

The women hugged.

"You *so* deserve it!" LaCroix added.

"God knows, I worked for it."

"You certainly did."

Meanwhile, Poblano was fidgeting with a pen inside his pants pocket, always uncomfortable in the presence of women emoting.

"So..." Davis recomposed herself. "After I finished writing that speech, I got dressed and rushed down here, fearing I had missed the whole thing. But lo and behold, I hadn't! Sorry

I couldn't have been at the cemetery. I'm not Catholic. So, I don't think I'd have cared for the Mass. But it's all so sad, really! Isn't it? Such a young man!"

"I should have called you," LaCroix said. "Sorry to put you through all this—all this anxiety."

"I *was* worried. Especially after I heard that you had quit the faculty."

Poblano perked up. He eyed LaCroix. *She'd quit the faculty?*

"I feared something terrible had happened," Davis raced on. "Well, of course, something terrible *had* happened. The kidnapping and all. But I mean something in addition to that. Something like…" She lowered her voice, "PTSD." She referred to post-traumatic stress disorder. "I feared you might have…"

"Lost my mind?" LaCroix giggled. "Well, I have news for *you*, Marla. I did lose my mind." She turned to Bachmann then winked at Davis. "We're getting married."

Davis gasped, displaying the fake astonishment people sometimes exhibit when something supposedly wonderful has happened, whether they consider it wonderful or not.

"We're thinking of a September wedding," Bachmann interjected.

"I… I'm so glad to hear this," Davis replied. "You two…" she looked at LaCroix then at Bachmann then back at LaCroix. "You two were so made for each other. I always thought so. But…" she turned to LaCroix with just the hint of a frown. "Did you really quit? I mean are you giving up…"

"My career?"

Davis nodded timidly.

"No, I'm not giving it up. I'm not *just* giving it up. I'm throwing it to the winds!"

Davis looked perplexed. "But... but your work... your research..."

"I have new work now." LaCroix turned to Bachmann, smiling up into his eyes. "Better work. Happier work."

He glanced at his gold watch. "I think perhaps we should be leaving now. Thank you again, detective. And, professor," he gave Davis a curt, little bow. "Congratulations!"

The lovebirds departed.

Steering among the tables, clearly eager to get away, they headed for the exit. Davis followed them out with her cosmeticized eyes, looking oddly lost for a moment, like a castaway on the shore of a desert island watching a ship sail into the distance toward the line between the ocean and the sky.

Suddenly, she turned to Poblano and produced a half-hearted smile. "Well! I guess I should be going too. Still so much work to do! I'll probably need to revise that speech. Polish it up a little. I always go for perfection, you know."

She turned her back on him and proceeded to find a path for herself amid the din of the crowd while Poblano lingered at the buffet table, watching her. Vaguely troubled, he tried to pinpoint the source of his discomfort. *There was something about her. Something off.*

He sifted through his recollections, disturbed by the sense that he'd overlooked something, a telling detail, a crucial connection, a significant missing link. *She had always seemed honest. She certainly paid well enough. If there was anything about her that aroused his suspicions, that made his detective's antennae quiver, he'd never noticed it until now. But now...*

He lifted a cookie from the table. A woman's arm passed under his. Startled, he turned to see his wife. Gloria smiled. "I think we should be going now, dear. The kids will be home soon."